Scripture quotations taken from the New American Standard
Bible® (NASB), Copyright © 1960, 1962, 1963, 1968, 1971, 1972,
1973, 1975, 1977, 1995 by The Lockman Foundation. Used by
permission. www.Lockman.org.

ISBN: 9781670949134

Dedication

For **Mom.** Watching all those Christmas romances would be way less fun without you. And for **Bruce,** who's a good sport to sit through every one of them with us. (And maybe, just maybe, you like them as much as Mom and I do.)

* * *

For **Trevor**, **Emily** and **Kristen** — our family lost you kiddos way too soon. I'm inspired by how bold you were — even at your young ages — in telling others of their need for Jesus. We love and miss you.

* * *

For **Jesus**, my Lord and Savior. May my words point people to you.

Purple Socks and Peppermint Tea

A Christmas Romance

Aunt Judy,
I wish I could hand
you this book in person.
Thank you for all your
love and support.
I love you!
Suzy
:)
Psalm 5:11-12

1

"Christopher Columbus!" Maribelle shouted as Santa smashed into her green-stockinged foot with a wham.

The ceramic Santa that she hauled out of storage at Bedford Books every December — along with all the other ancient decorations — had broken free of his cardboard prison, and her foot bore the brunt of his revolt. This wasn't the fat man's first escape attempt, but it was the first time he didn't have a softish surface to break his fall.

This time it was fatal.

Santa was beside himself.

And on top of himself. And, well … all around himself.

Santa was everywhere — but not in that "Santa can circle the globe in one night" kind of way.

Santa was smashed.

Maribelle sighed.

She was more annoyed at jolly ol' St. Nick for dashing himself to bits than she was sad to see him go. In fact, if her right foot hadn't been throbbing from the blow, she might have booted him the rest of the way into oblivion, past her wet shoes, out the back door of the bookstore and into the alleyway. He already had a skinned-up face; why had the Hatches kept him around all these years, anyway?

As that thought came to mind, though, just as quickly a sweet Christmas carol pushed it away. *"God Rest You, Merry Gentlemen — really?"* Maribelle muttered to herself as the lyric "tidings of comfort and joy" flitted across her conscience.

She supposed it was because she had been a bit miffed at God lately, and God was chiding her for being such a sour pickle.

He often interrupted her self-centered meanderings by bringing snippets of songs to her. Or sometimes Bible verses she had learned as a child. Or maybe a quote from the saintly Mother Teresa — anything to make her feel guilty for being a Scrooge at "the most wonderful time of the year."

Usually Maribelle could handle the holiday merriment. She would just put on a close-lipped smile to hide her gritted teeth and go with the flow. Parties? Plastic smile. Family gatherings? At least there would always be Nanny's strawberry cake — her favorite. (If her mom didn't make the cake, one of Mom's sisters would; otherwise there would be a revolt, or at least a heated "conversation" about whose turn it had been to bring the cake.) Maribelle could even halfway enjoy herself at the family events, as long as no one hassled her about her bare wedding-ring finger and lack of a mate.

Maribelle's heartbreak was supposed to be ancient history by now, but she just didn't seem to be able to get past it. She knew that the breakup had been for the best, but the pain was still raw at the oddest times, even now, two years after her fiancé dumped her. Maribelle had prayed not to become bitter, and she supposed the Lord's grace and mercy were the only things standing between her and total despair. She was immensely grateful for that.

But the older cousin who inevitably grabbed her left hand at holiday get-togethers and examined her ring finger, raising his eyebrows with that unspoken jab, "You're over 30, Maribelle. When are you going to give your parents some grandchildren?" ... well, this Christmas she would have to pray a lot to keep from punching him in the eggnoggin. Usually she tried to play along with his little attempt at "humor," but it had been getting harder and harder, especially since her epic failure in the engagement department.

Yes, this year, faking holiday cheer seemed a bit too much to ask. Sometimes she even wondered why people celebrated Christmas. The older she got, the more friends and family she heard about who were going through painful experiences, whether those were health crises, relationship problems, depression (not uncommon this time of year) or sometimes unspeakable tragedy. Why didn't everyone just crawl under the covers and stay there between Halloween and January 2?

But even though she had grown cynical about the holiday and outwardly grumbled at the season's festivities, she secretly bristled at the injustice of a small family business being put on the defensive at Christmastime — when its owners and staff should have nothing heavier on their minds than handing out Clem's famous Jingle Bell Hot Chocolate and bear hugs with abandon.

Just the thought of the bookstore's misfortunes sent a chill up her spine. Maribelle hadn't turned up the thermostat yet this morning, but it didn't matter. Nothing could help her shake that chill.

As store manager, Maribelle typically arrived at the old storefront business on Bailey Street at least an hour before anyone else, and that meant two hours before Bedford Books opened at 9. She always had one part-time staff member arrive an hour early to help her get the place ready for business. The owners were getting up in years and, though the Hatches still had a strong work ethic, it was harder for them on the more frigid mornings to get to the store as early as Maribelle.

Besides, she was an early riser, and she reveled in the crisp weather. It made her feel alive, even when other parts of her life made her feel dead inside.

As she turned up the heat and went to the closet for the broom and dustpan, she tried to hold back tears, but the pain in her foot and the prospect of losing the store — her happy place — made her stop in her tracks and put all of her effort into holding back the ugly-cry.

The faint scent of peppermint wafted over to her just in time. She paused for a moment, closed her eyes and savored the lingering aroma. She had sipped on peppermint tea last night as she looked over the store's balance sheet, and 12 hours later she could almost taste the sweet indulgence again; the memory — and the scent — helped her perk up enough to move on and get back to the business at hand.

The Hatches had built a beautiful little sanctuary at Bedford Books. In fact, "business," while necessary to keep the doors open, wasn't the primary word most people would use to describe the store.

Clem and Ginnie not only treated their staff like family, their customers were the recipients of the couple's warmth and kindness, as well.

People didn't come here just to buy books. They came to sit and chat — or read — in the cozy alcove, to sip coffee or tea (on the house), to see their friends, to experience story hour with their children and to participate in a myriad of other rituals that created a living, breathing community.

In her time off, when it was just Maribelle and her cat, Dickens, in their cozy apartment, she would much rather have her nose in a book — a good, old-fashioned classic like *Little Women* (where she got some of her pet phrases) — than decorate the store for Christmas.

But she couldn't deny that she loved the Bedford microculture. She had made real friends here — children and their parents and grands, college students, business professionals, intellectuals, authors, visitors from other cities — and she was grateful she had found a home away from home in this little section of town.

* * *

Part of the reason Maribelle's chest tightened when she thought about the store's future is that Clement and Virginia Hatch had put their confidence in her when she had no experience as a store manager. The Hatches were firm believers in people — a confidence that had grown since the early days of the bookstore and one reason they believed they could trust Maribelle in her new role.

Both raised with strict boundaries and a strong work ethic, Clem and Ginnie had a foundation of two previous generations of ownership of Bedford Books, and with each generation the business had gotten stronger and more firmly established in the community.

Until recently.

The community status was still strong, but the financial picture had started to fray around the edges.

When Virginia's grandfather Arthur, at the urging of his best friend, Cletus, decided to establish the business, he refused to take on debt to get things going. Cletus, Clem's grandfather, was wealthy and had never had a need to borrow money. After much debate, Arthur allowed Cletus to provide the funds, and they bought the building that still housed the store to this day.

Cletus had hired an accountant to take care of the financial side of the business, but he left the everyday decisions and operations to Arthur.

By the time Ginnie and Clem inherited the bookstore from their families, business was booming. It didn't hurt that they were the only ones who carried certain categories of books in the area. They specialized in volumes of local interest, supported local authors and hosted book signings, children's events and fun-but-educational workshops regularly.

People loved the Hatches, and Clem and Ginnie loved them back — almost as much as they loved each other.

But times change, and technology required Bedford Books to adapt or go under.

E-books had taken a large chunk of business away from the store, so they had decided to host an e-book seller and app on their website. They'd had to hire a tech geek to set up and operate the website. The owners were intelligent people, but there was only so much bandwidth in their brains to learn all the new technology, run the store and have any semblance of a life outside of work.

In their younger days, they could have pulled it off. Now, they were tired and had begun relying on others for many things they used to do without a thought.

Including someone to take a look at the store's financials.

As the young store manager visually assessed the front counter, making sure the little red pencil cup of multicolored candy sticks was full, the cardholder held plenty of bookmarks and the basket of stocking stuffers overflowed with fuzzy Christmas critters, a little dancing prism of light caught her eye.

She pushed up her wire-rimmed glasses and watched. A sunbeam seemed to pirouette around the countertop. She looked across the room to see where the little scene originated. There it was! It was the delicate glass bell that hung from a silver thread in one of the front windows. When the heater kicked on, the warm breath from the vent caused the small iridescent bell to twirl gently in its wake.

For a moment, Maribelle was transfixed. Her heart rate slowed, and her shoulders relaxed. The little scene was pure magic, and it made her forget her troubles, if only for a few moments.

Too often lately, she had been so preoccupied she failed to notice such tiny wonders — such "tidings of comfort and joy" that the Lord kept sending her way, despite her grumpiness.

It was a small and momentary thing, yes, but she used to marvel at so many little things that most people overlooked. But now, she had grown accustomed to barreling through life, shutting out — deliberately or not — the things that used to make her smile, if even for just a moment.

Why had she let herself become so cynical? How had she allowed the little things to lose their magic?

As she went to straighten the display of children's holiday books near the door, Maribelle resolved to work on her attitude, despite what was going on behind the scenes at Bedford Books. No one likes a year-round Scrooge, and Christmas was definitely not the time to be a crab cake, a grinchy-grinch. Or, as her mother would say: a Negative Noelly.

When she was a little girl, Christmas couldn't come fast enough. She wasn't the typical kid on Santa's knee with a mile-long list, though. She had always been more interested in the caroling, the cookies, the decorations, the TV specials. Even the church pageant — where she was perennially tasked with the famous angelic annunciation because none of the other kids could memorize the passage from Luke 2 — held more interest for her than shiny packages under the tree.

Maribelle had always been a bit different.

And suddenly a memory stopped her dead in her tracks.

As she paused her tidying, she remembered a story that Clem had told her several years ago about the ceramic Santa that had just bit the dust.

Clem's grandmother had received the Santa when his mother was a girl, and she passed it down to her only daughter when she married and had children of her own. Mother kept it wrapped in a soft scarf and would gently take it out each December and place it on the mantel. Clem remembered because this iridescent piece of Christmas lore was his mother's favorite memento from her own childhood, and she would talk about it with anyone who paused to comment on it. Each year, Santa Claus perched high upon the mantel, as though he were watching over the family as the busy holiday season ramped up.

One December, just after Clem turned 7, he was in the living room practicing kamikaze dives with his wooden airplane while his mother tended to the laundry in the garage. Santa, sitting a bit too close to the edge of the mantel, skittered off as the plane swooped in for a crash-landing. As Santa commenced his own suicide attempt, Clem caught him in the nick of time. Well, almost: St. Nick skimmed the coffee table on the way down, and Clem scooped him up just in time to keep him from hitting the floor.

For the rest of his life, Santa had a skinned nose, despite Clem's best efforts to hide the evidence of his crime.

After such a close call, Clem was so shaken he never took his warplanes near the living room again. That was voluntary; the punishment from his father was … well, a little more like a prison sentence. He made Clem chop wood for the stove every day for the next month. Clemmie's 30-day haul pretty much ensured that their woodpile was set for the rest of the winter.

The first time Clem told that story in Maribelle's presence, she was a bit horrified. His father's punishment of 7-year-old Clem seemed harsh — quite extreme for the crime. But Maribelle hadn't understood the sentimental value of the holiday figure, and still didn't — until Santa was gone.

Maribelle's face felt hot. How could she have regarded someone else's prized possession with such a cavalier attitude?

Now she dreaded telling Clem the truth about Santa.

But she must.

It was a double-whammy for this week: First, she'd had to give her employers the bad news about the store's finances. Now, she'd have to tell Clem that she had destroyed his beloved family treasure.

And with Christmas only three weeks away.

2

Within 15 seconds of the loud crash, six of Joel Stewart's seven co-workers were huddled around him in his small office, trying to avoid stepping on huge shards of glass.

"Are you OK, Joel?" said his assistant, Elizabeth, watching wide-eyed as the accountant reached for a towel from his gym bag to try to keep the blood from staining his lavender dress shirt and purple necktie — or the brand new cream-and-beige area rug.

"What happened?" said Kaitlyn, whose desk was near Joel's office. "It sounded like you fell through the roof!"

Joel laughed, which was a huge mistake, because it made him ease off the pressure he was holding on his right forearm. Blood gushed from the wound, and one of the office assistants thought she might faint from the sight of it.

"Well, first, I think I need to get to the emergency room. Can someone drive me? I'll explain on the way to the hospital. This cut seems to be kinda deep."

Joel, standing there bleeding, was a bit annoyed that he had to point out the obvious. And accountants were supposed to be details people.

Stepping cautiously around the broken glass, Andre grabbed another clean towel and tightened it around the upper part of Joel's right arm, then took his friend's good arm and navigated him toward the door.

"Kandis, would you grab Joel's coat and his cell phone while I grab mine from my office? Keep pressure on that arm, Joel. I'll meet you in the reception area in a minute."

As Kandis gathered Joel's belongings and escorted him out to meet Andre, the others began picking up the pieces of tempered glass that, until five minutes ago, had been Joel's fanciest office furnishing.

The small accounting firm had struggled for the past few years, experiencing one setback after another — unfortunate hiring decisions, an ill-advised marketing campaign that had made Goldman & Blackburn the laughingstock of the local industry association, even a lawsuit from a disgruntled client (who was now serving a 15-year prison term). They just hadn't been able to catch a break, and for too long the office always seemed to be in crisis mode — until recently.

* * *

Since the beginning of the year, and especially once the frenzied pace of tax season had passed, things had started to settle into a nice rhythm.

No one was calling in "sick," employee interaction was becoming more pleasant again — conversational rather than borderline confrontational — the firm had landed a big client, profits had jumped accordingly and the boss had made a couple of decisions that put everyone in a chipper mood.

"First off," Kim began, "this firm is starting to look more like the company that Dad and his best friend established 45 years ago." She looked around the conference room at the faces she had grown to love since she took over after her father's death 10 years earlier.

"And it's about time. We've had to overcome a lot these past few years. You don't know what your loyalty has meant to me. Although, I must say, a few mornings I woke up afraid I might discover a mutiny when I arrived at the office."

The group laughed at the joke, but no one contradicted Kim. Most of the staff was simply thankful the atmosphere had improved and that coming to work was bearable again — even fun at times.

She continued.

"So, because we've had three positive quarters in a row, and because you've all been troupers and have stuck with me throughout so much uncertainty, you'll all be getting Christmas bonuses this year!"

That brought a loud collective cheer. It had been three years since the last bonuses of any kind.

"Also, in time for Christmas, we're going to spend a little money upgrading this tired old space. There's enough in the budget for each of you to have $700 to decorate your office spaces as you please — within reason, of course. No psychedelic sofas or moose heads on the walls. You get what I mean. This is a dignified accounting firm, after all."

Another round of laughter and a few minutes of chatter about this positive turn of events, and soon it was back to daily business. But the announcements had lightened the mood of Goldman & Blackburn Accounting, and the hum of productivity was accompanied by smiles rather than furrowed brows. The holiday season at G&B would be joyful again this year.

(What Kim hadn't said was that the decorating stipends meant she wouldn't take home a paycheck in December; business had been good this year, but not *that* good. She still wanted to exercise caution. Nevertheless, she felt that her employees deserved a reward for their loyalty — and the workspaces did need a bit of sprucing up. Christmas had always put her in a joyful mood, even when times were hard, and she wanted the workplace atmosphere to match that spirit.)

✳ ✳ ✳

No sooner had Joel finally settled into liking his fancy new glass table — with no small bit of convincing from Elizabeth, who had picked it out — than it all came crashing down.

It was a good thing he had Andre around to pick up the pieces.

Andre had always been the take-charge guy at the office. He not only had a generous and humble spirit, volunteering to do grunt work when the situation called for it (even though he ranked second-highest in seniority at the firm), he never waited for someone to call on him before he sprang into action.

His can-do nature was a large part of the reason the firm was still in business.

So, while Joel was getting his forearm stitched up in the ER, Andre was on his cell making sure the glass-tastrophe was being taken care of back in Joel's office.

"I want you to call Raylene's Cleaning Machine and get someone from Ray's crew to make sure all the broken glass is gone from Joel's office before he gets back," Andre told Elizabeth. "She cleans my house a few times a year, and I had a similar situation a couple of years back. When Raylene and her crew were done, not a speck of glass could be found. I'll text you Ray's contact info."

"Andre, how do you always know the right thing to do?" Elizabeth said. "While everyone else stood around and stared at Joel and the broken glass, you took charge. You created a tourniquet for Joel's arm, you got him out the door and to the hospital, and now you're ordering a cleaning service for him."

"Lizzie, my friend, it's not that hard. It was pretty obvious what needed to be done. If we had stood around and debated what to do, Joel could have bled to death!"

Elizabeth's heart seized at the thought. She had worked for Joel for eight of her 10 years at the firm, and the young woman had grown to look at her boss as a trusted mentor and friend.

"What exactly happened, anyway?" she asked Andre. "One minute I'm pouring myself a cup of coffee, and the next minute I hear a loud crash. And then the whole office is running toward Joel's office like the place is on fire!"

Andre laughed, but he chose his next words carefully.

"He tripped over something."

"Tripped over what?" Lizzie asked. Then, before Andre could answer, "Isn't tempered glass supposed to be shatter-proof?"

"It's much stronger than regular glass, but, no, it's not shatter-proof. And Joel fell pretty hard. He thinks the metal tumbler he was holding slammed into the table first and cracked it, and that set things in motion."

Again, Lizzie asked what caused Joel's tumble.

Why can't she just leave that alone? Andre thought.

He hadn't planned to tell her, but she was persistent. Besides, their co-workers would want every detail, and Elizabeth would find out eventually, despite his best efforts to keep the real story from her.

"He tripped over the golf clubs."

"Oh!" Lizzie exclaimed. She fought back tears. Elizabeth had saved all year to buy her boyfriend, Rick, a used set of golf clubs. When she finally found the perfect set and made the purchase, she didn't know what to do with them. She had a tiny apartment and no place to hide the clubs when Rick visited, so she had asked Joel to keep them in his office until Christmas Eve. While the fresh coat of paint was curing from Joel's remodel, they had decided to lay the clubs on the floor rather than lean them upright against a wall.

And now her gift had caused serious injury to her boss.

"I don't know what to say," Elizabeth cried. "I feel terrible!"

Elizabeth was almost afraid to ask the next question, but she had to know.

"Is Joel ... mad at me?" And, before Andre could open his mouth to answer, she corrected herself. "Actually, that's a selfish question. The first thing I should have asked is, will Joel really be OK? Tell me the truth: How serious is his injury? What can I do?"

Her thoughts tumbled out in a jumble of questions and emotions.

"First thing you can do is stop feeling guilty. It wasn't your fault," Andre assured Lizzie. "Joel doesn't blame you — at all. In fact, he made me promise that if you found out how this happened, I'd make you understand that you weren't to blame.

"Joel's arm will take some time to heal — it was a pretty deep cut, but it could have been worse," Andre continued. "He'll be OK."

Elizabeth was relieved. Sort of. She would feel guilty for a while, but she was glad Joel didn't blame her. That was just like him.

Joel wasn't the type to hold grudges or assign blame. He believed that things happened for a reason, even when people couldn't understand those reasons — maybe never would — and that everything would work out in the end.

Joel was an optimist, and he was always trying to get Lizzie to stop worrying and find the joy in life.

It took practice, but Joel's attitude was starting to rub off on his assistant.

But today's events had challenged that train of thought.

While Joel's co-workers waited for word on the seriousness of his wound, Kandis was in her office staring out the window at the light snow. The gray day didn't help the gloomy feeling she'd had since the accident.

She knew Joel's injury wasn't life-threatening, but the experience had jolted her into a pensive state. It had got her to start thinking of things she normally tried to keep below the surface.

Lots of people wait until a crisis to declare their feelings for someone. She liked to think of herself as atypical, but maybe she wasn't.

She liked to think of herself as brave — and she was, in most situations — but when it came to her emotions, she usually held them close.

She liked to think of herself as independent, strong and capable of navigating life in her own way, on her own terms. No partner needed, no close connections necessary, not even a cat to keep her company at home.

But maybe she wasn't any of those things. Maybe she was needier than she let on, even to herself.

As she twisted a lock of red hair, she debated:

Is now the time to tell Joel how I feel?

What if he doesn't feel the same? We work together. It would be so awkward in the office. I'd have to quit my job. Maybe I would drive him away and he would quit his job. Maybe we'd both quit our jobs and find new ones. What if we ended up at the same new place?

What if he laughs in my face???

Or maybe (probably not, but maybe) he does feel the same and we started dating.

What if Kim found out and fired us both?

What if, what if, what if?

"Kandis, phone call from your brother. Line 2. Can you take it?" Kandis' assistant, Terrance, interrupted her tortured train of thought to bring her back to reality.

"Um, yeah. I'll take it," she replied, half-annoyed and half-grateful for the interruption to the unproductive loop her mind had been stuck in.

Tucking the stray strand of hair behind her ear, she put on her headset and punched the blinking light.

"Hey, bro," Kandis greeted her brother.

"What's shakin', bacon?" Kurtis said to his twin, who was older by two minutes yet always acted like she had two years on him.

"Mom wants us both for dinner tonight. Can you make it?"

"What's the occasion?" Kandis asked.

"Nothing special. She just wants to be sure she doesn't forget what you look like. And she knows you'll beg off when the Christmas parties get into full swing. She wants a quiet evening to catch up with her kids."

"You know I have to attend some of those parties, Kurtis," his sister replied. "It's not like I enjoy it."

"I do know. And Mom knows. Like I said, she wants some of your time before you get too busy. She's not trying to make you feel guilty."

"Is that why she made you call me instead of doing it herself?"

"She didn't *make* me call you. I volunteered. But, yeah, she was afraid you'd say no if the invitation came directly from her," Kurtis said. "She's been very vulnerable since Dad died. And she's lonely, sis. Give her a break."

"I guess you're right. I have declined a few of her invites lately. Tell her I'll be there.

"Better yet," Kandis said. "I'll call her, myself."

Feeling vulnerable can cause a person to react in two ways: Either you become more generous with your loved ones, or you push them away.

In Kandis' case, Joel's unfortunate run-in with his glass table kindled a longing for time with family that she hadn't felt in a while.

The awareness that Christmas was just around the corner only intensified her desire to reconnect.

3

"Ginnie, do you know where the Christmas cards are?" Bethany had asked the store owner a day after ceramic Santa's early-morning ride into oblivion, sans sleigh.

Bethany worked part time and, when she didn't have her nose in the latest murder mystery, she was in charge of the store's correspondence. She called herself the Composer in Chief. Any outgoing mail that wasn't accounting related got Bethany's personal touch on a piece of the store's friendly stationery or greeting cards they had printed — locally, of course.

"I don't know, B.B. Are you sure we haven't run out of them?" Ginnie replied. Bethany may have titled herself Composer in Chief, but her co-workers had given her a different nickname: Bethany Bookworm. It started as a joke, but, before long, everyone had started calling her B.B. She considered it a term of endearment and secretly loved it when another member of the team referred to her in that way.

"Seems to me that last December we got down to the last box and someone was supposed to add it to the to-do list for this fall to order more," the storeowner said.

"Well, if that's the case, they didn't do it. Was that my job?" Bethany said. "I hope not, but I guess it doesn't matter now. We need to get an order in right away — like, *yesterday*."

"Go ahead and place the order, B.B. You probably should order an extra box or two this time, though. Figure out how many we used last year, and add at least 25 cards to that number. Bedford Printing is on speed dial on the office phone.

"OK, Gin —"

"Oh, and Bethany?" Ginnie interrupted. "If they have any pretty cards with the Baby Jesus on them, let's get those. We got a little too

Santa Clausy with the last batch of cards. I want people to remember why we celebrate Christmas."

"Gotcha," Bethany said.

As she walked to the back of the store to call the print shop, she began whistling "Sweet Little Jesus Boy," hoping it wasn't too sacrilegious to whistle such a reverent song.

* * *

"Are you sure about that? Could you check again?"

Bethany was only mildly concerned that the Bedford Graphics & Printing manager refused to place an order for Christmas cards on credit. She knew there had to be a mistake.

"I don't have to check, Bethany. Everyone here is well aware of the past-due status of the bookstore's account," said Jubilee, a longtime employee of the printshop.

"I'm sorry, I don't mean to be rude," Bethany replied. "It's just that … that doesn't sound right. Clem and Ginnie have always prided themselves on paying their bills on time. The only places they buy anything on credit are the printshop and the bakery, and that's for 30 days only."

"I know that's how things used to be, but since Maribelle started doing the books, that's not the way it has been," Jubilee said.

"Oh. Well, OK. I'll talk to Maribelle and see what we need to do."

"Bring the account up to date; that's what you need to do. And any future orders — at least for the time being — are gonna need to be paid upfront," the manager said.

"OK." Bethany's voice was small as the printshop manager's words sank in.

"I'm not trying to be unkind, sweetie. But our notices to the store and our phone calls have gone unreturned for too long. In fact, my next step was going to be a personal visit with Clem. I know he's the one who did the bookkeeping until the beginning of the year."

"Thanks, ma'am. Someone will be in touch."

Bethany hung up and went to find Maribelle at the front of the store.

"Mare, could I talk to you for a minute? In the back?" Bethany said.

"What's up, B.B.?" Maribelle said.

Bethany scrunched her brow and said, "Let's talk in the office."

As Maribelle and Bethany stepped over a string of Christmas lights on the floor just outside the office, Bethany pondered what she was going to say. She decided to take Maribelle's usual approach and just spill it.

"I just got off the phone with Jubilee," Bethany began. "She says our account is past due and they won't fill any more orders until we bring it current."

"What?" Maribelle was incredulous. "There has to be some mistake. I don't know about any past-due bills."

"That's what I thought," the young woman replied. "Apparently it's several months old. My first thought was that maybe in the transition from Clem to you, something got overlooked. But Jubilee said they've sent us mail and had phone calls go unreturned. Do you know anything about that?"

"No! That just can't be right. Are you sure she was talking about Bedford Books? Maybe she pulled up the wrong account."

"Positive," Bethany said. "She even mentioned you and Clem as the ones who handle the bookkeeping. Maribelle ..."

"Yes? Spit it out, Bethany."

"She seemed to imply that everything was fine until you took over the books."

"Hmmm. Well, don't you worry. I'll look into it," Maribelle told her. "I'll take a look at the ledger and talk to Clem when he gets in after lunch. Then one of us will call Jubilee and straighten things out."

"OK, Mare. Let me know if there's anything I can do to help."

"Thanks, Beebs. I'll let you know. But don't worry; it'll be all right."

With that, Bethany went back to sorting through the light strings for burned-out bulbs and Maribelle closed the office door and planted herself at the desk, muttering to herself about bills and books and bank accounts.

✻ ✻ ✻

Before Maribelle settled in to examine the store's accounts-payable records, she realized she would need a cup of peppermint tea first. It would boost her mood and help keep her alert.

She didn't want to miss anything. Besides, it rankled her that Jubilee would imply any sort of misdeeds on her part, and her reputation was at stake.

At Christmastime, peppermint tea was more popular with store employees and customers, so Maribelle kept her own little secret stash in the office. She would hate to run out in the middle of a stressful situation, so she had brought a little blue and silver tin from home and filled it with plenty of tea bags and a few peppermint sticks for any type of Christmas crisis.

She called it her emergency tea party in a tin, and she was the only one who knew it was there.

She sat in the old green-leather office chair and opened the bottom-right drawer of the wood desk that had belonged to Virginia's grandfather. As she dug behind the hanging file folders, feeling around for the cool metal of her emergency tea party, Maribelle discovered a different box — one she didn't recall ever seeing before.

It was a little bigger than her tea box, and instead of blue and silver, this one was green and white with faded cherubs floating all around. It looked like a vintage tin from Victorian days, if such a thing existed back then, and it was tied tightly with a pale pink satin ribbon.

Maribelle placed the tin onto the desk blotter. Besides being a bit larger, this one was a lot heavier than the one that held her tea bags and peppermint sticks.

She untied the bow and opened it.

Inside she found the tin crammed full of papers, so many that she knew the owner would have had to work hard to close the lid and get it to stay shut. Hence, the ribbon, she supposed.

As Maribelle pushed her glasses up on her nose and started unfolding the papers, she realized that most of the papers were invoices.

Invoices from the office supply store, from the office equipment supplier, from the pest-control service, from the secretary of state (tax-related letters) ... and, yes, from Bedford Graphics & Printing.

"What in the world?" Maribelle whispered to the empty office.

These bills were months old — things she should have been aware of but, she had to admit, she wasn't.

Since Clem had shifted the bookkeeping responsibilities to Maribelle in the new year, when he said he wanted to work fewer hours, she had a list of vendors to pay. Some of them were online payments, and others — apparently all of these — were invoiced by paper and sent via the postal system.

Without a background in accounting or in any type of retail management, she just hadn't thought about some of these expenses. She should have.

She had been flattered, grateful and overwhelmed when Clem and Ginnie asked her to manage the store. At first it was just ordering books, hiring and managing the employees and their schedules and being the face people saw first thing when the store opened.

But the list of responsibilities had begun to grow, along with Maribelle's stress level.

She was going to need to buy stock in the peppermint tea company.

* * *

By the time she finished looking over the contents of the green and white tin, Maribelle was in a mild state of shock.

The invoices she found represented several thousand dollars worth of unpaid bills. It was a wonder the store was still operating. As she thought about it, though, she realized that she *had* been receiving the utility bills. If she hadn't, she probably would have been suspicious. Maybe not at first, but it would have dawned on her — eventually — that she hadn't been receiving invoices for something as basic as keeping the lights and water on at the store.

Many of the other bills, though, were ones she wouldn't necessarily have missed as an inexperienced store manager. She hadn't been schooled in tax law or standard accounting practices, nor were some of the behind-the-scenes expenses of running a store obvious to her.

No, there was just too much to learn in her first few months as manager to realize that some things were just not right.

Such as a green and white tin crammed with unpaid bills.

How had the Bedford Graphics & Printing owners kept from serving the bookstore some type of legal notice?

Or maybe they had.

She took another look, then a third look — just to be certain — through the papers in the tin and, nope, nothing resembling a legal threat could be found. She supposed the good relationship Bedford Books and Bedford Printing had enjoyed over the years had something to do with the goodwill the bookstore had been fortunate to receive from the printshop. But wow. Not everyone would have extended such grace to a business that had fallen so behind in payments.

Maribelle's slight headache was turning into a full-blown migraine. She was getting nauseated just thinking about the implications of the papers she had found.

Who had hidden these away? What were they trying to hide, exactly? Was someone stealing from the store? Was there some type of embezzlement scheme going on?

Maribelle didn't even know enough about bookkeeping to know what might be going on — or even what questions to ask.

She'd better go find Clem and Ginnie.

❋ ❋ ❋

When Maribelle emerged from the office, she went to look for Ginnie and found her behind the old oak counter, talking to a customer. Maribelle didn't want to disturb her, so she sought out Clem.

She found him in the children's section, straightening the tiny primary-colored chairs that went with the little round table he had built with his own hands for the store's littlest patrons.

Clem loved children, and Maribelle never ceased to be moved by his attention to detail when it came to things he thought would put smiles on their sweet little faces. Years earlier, when Ginnie had started talking about ordering a little table for the children's area, Clem wouldn't hear of it. He wanted to put his personal touch on at least one permanent fixture for the children. It was one more way for him to show love to the little tykes, especially for those whose home lives were less than ideal.

Some of the kids came only to browse, to sit at the little table and thumb through the treasures; their parents couldn't afford to buy them books. Or they came to story time and left, but they never left empty-handed. Clem always bought an extra copy of one special book in each new order, and he kept it in a secret stash on a shelf in the office. If a child was especially needy (and not greedy), he'd wait until a private moment and give the youngster a book he knew would be loved and cherished.

"The book company sent an extra in our last order, and I'd like you to have it," Clem would whisper. It wasn't really a lie, and he loved the smiles those "book company extras" induced.

When children were in the store, for Clem it was almost as if they were on stage — like when the lights go down and the spotlight shines on a particular, solo character who's about to perform a soliloquy. The audience sees only that lone character, as if he or she is the only one on earth for those few, precious minutes.

That's how Clem saw the children.

When they were around, their needs — even their wants — came before anything else. He went out of his way for them and never seemed to tire of coming up with new ideas to delight them.

Until lately.

Clem seemed to be less energetic than he had been just a few months ago. Still, there he was, fussing over the little corner that was dedicated to his favorite visitors. It seemed to perk him up in the

21

moments that would exhaust anyone else — especially Maribelle, who seemed to be perpetually exhausted these days.

Maribelle paused for a moment to watch Clem work, humming a medley of Christmas songs as he stood admiring the little nook that was the perfect size for the eager future readers.

Clem and the children shared a special bond, and it was one of Maribelle's greatest pleasures to watch them greet one another when the kids would arrive at Bedford Books.

The shy ones would return Clem's wave tentatively at first, then warm up to him once he had earned their trust.

He was so gentle and patient with them.

And the bolder, more outgoing children would run up to Clem and give him bear hugs.

One little boy, a 6-year-old brainiac named Trevor, nearly knocked Clem down when he ran to greet his old friend one day. When Clem regained his balance, he and Trevor laughed like it had been a game.

Trevor's older brother, Lucas, was also whip-smart, and he liked to see if he could stump Clem on the latest exciting thing Lucas had learned in home-school or in the treasures he took home from Bedford Books. Clem and Lucas had learned so much from each other; Maribelle knew that their special friendship would last a lifetime.

Unfortunately, Trevor's lifetime was short. The entire store mourned when the boy was diagnosed with cancer at age 8 and lost his battle within a year. They had no doubt Trevor was better off, because he had given his heart to Jesus at a young age. He was known for telling people that they needed to "get right or get left," as he liked to put it. Trevor's philosophy was that no one ever knew when their time would be up, so they'd better be ready to meet Jesus. He was serious about that, and he never missed an opportunity to share his faith and urge people to turn to the Lord.

Trevor, Lucas and all the other children who visited Bedford Books were a delight in every way to Clem, and Maribelle took delight in observing them together.

As Maribelle replayed those memories, she hated to return to reality, but she needed answers.

"Hey, Clem!"

"Yes, my dear. How's it going?"

"I don't mean to interrupt, but I have a couple of things to talk to you about."

She debated about which to bring up first: the fact that she had smashed ceramic Santa to smithereens or the discovery she had just made in the desk drawer. She decided that the invoice situation was more serious, so she went for it.

"First, I have some questions for you about the bills," she began hesitantly.

Clem paused his arranging and looked at Maribelle.

"What about the bills?"

"Well ..." Maribelle wasn't sure where to start. The whole thing seemed odd to her. Then again, there had to be a logical explanation, and letting her imagination run wild wouldn't get her the answers she needed.

"Ummm ..."

She wouldn't start with the overdue bills at the printshop; she would ease into that. But how?

"Well, Clem ... I ..."

"What is it, dear heart? Just spit it out."

OK, enough hemming and hawing. She was a direct person, even with those she loved.

"Clem, I found a green and white tin in the back of a drawer in the office. I was looking for my tin of peppermint tea and ran across it in the bottom of the drawer where I keep my secret tea stash."

"Oh?" Clem's face lit up. There was a gleam of mischief in his eyes. "Was it a secret stash of chocolate?"

Maribelle's shoulders relaxed. At least Clem didn't seem to know about the tin. Did she think he would? What had she been thinking?

She had to admit to herself that Clem would be the most likely person to know about the collection of bills hidden in a desk drawer in his own office — in his own business. He had been the one keeping the books for many years before Maribelle, after all.

"No, Clem, it was a bunch of unpaid bills. *Past due* bills," she emphasized.

"That can't be right."

"That's what I thought," Maribelle said. "But I looked over each piece of paper and made sure I wasn't imagining things — that they're all from this year and that I haven't paid them. In fact, I've never seen the names of some of the vendors."

Now it was Clem's turn to furrow his brow.

"Why would someone hide them in a drawer? Are you sure they haven't been paid?"

"I can't be 100 percent certain without looking at the ledger, but some were accompanied by notices from the vendors saying second and third notices. I had actually gone into the office to look at the ledger, but when I found the tin I thought I'd better talk to you first."

"I need to sit down," Clem said. "This just doesn't sound right. Who would hide a bunch of bills in the back of a drawer?"

"That's what I was hoping you could tell me. As far as I know, only you handled the books before you gave me the responsibility almost a year ago."

"Let's go take a look," Clem said. "I need to see what you're talking about."

4

Maribelle led Clem to the green and white tin in the office. Before going to look for him, she had placed it back in the drawer where she found it. No sense alerting anyone else right now — especially when she didn't know who had hidden the papers.

And one question had been nagging at Maribelle. If someone was trying to steal from the store — and she still wasn't sure how — why would he or she leave evidence *at* the store? Why not take it home, or burn it, shred it or otherwise erase its existence?

She supposed that was one thing they would find out when they started looking into the mystery.

As she took the tin from the drawer and handed it to Clem, she watched his reaction.

Was that a glimmer of recognition? Of guilt?

Immediately she felt ashamed that the possibility had even crossed her mind.

Clem would never do anything crooked. She had known him and Ginnie for years, and they were well-known in the community for their integrity and forthrightness. Besides that, if he were going to do something shady with his own business' accounting records, it would be really odd to do it this way.

But who could've done it?

Clem opened the tin and gasped at the volume of papers inside.

As he started sorting through, he said, "Sweetie, why would anyone hide all these in here? I just don't get it."

"I don't, either, Clem. That's why I came to talk to you and Ginnie. She was busy with a customer, so I came to you first."

"So you haven't told her?"

"No, she doesn't know a thing."

"Well, we'd better go get her. She needs to know right away," Clem said. "And maybe she'll have better answers than we're coming up with. She's always been better at figuring out puzzles than I have."

Maribelle left the room and went to find Ginnie. Without explaining what was going on, she asked Ginnie to meet her in the office. But, first, Maribelle wanted to see who else was in the store. Which employees were there, and exactly where were they? No sense alerting the staff until she and the owners knew more. And she certainly didn't want any customers to suspect that something was wrong.

When she was satisfied that their private meeting would, indeed, be private, she went back to the office and closed the door behind her.

Ginnie was sitting at the desk and looking up at Clem over her reading glasses.

"I don't understand," Ginnie said. "Why would anyone hide a bunch of old bills in the back of a drawer in our desk? And *who* would do it?"

"That's exactly what Clem and I are wondering, Ginnie." Maribelle was starting to get a sense of deja vu.

"Have you looked at the ledger?" she asked Maribelle.

"Not yet," Maribelle replied. "I was about to do that when I found the tin of papers. And there's more, Ginnie. The whole reason I came in here to look at the books is that Bethany called Jubilee to order more Christmas cards, and Jubilee told her we needed to bring our account current. She said they had been sending notices and that they wouldn't do any more business with us on credit — it would have to be cash only."

"That's crazy," Ginnie said. "You've been paying the bills, haven't you?"

"Well, the ones I knew about, yes. But I wasn't aware of all these that I found today," Maribelle said.

The novice store manager was near tears. She loved her employers and had enjoyed their respect for many years — as evidenced by her promotion almost a year ago — and it pained her to think that they might suspect her of wrongdoing. After all, she was the one who had found the tin of papers. But perhaps they thought her "discovery" was a convenient coverup in light of Bethany's conversation with the printshop employee.

Maybe they would think Maribelle decided to "find" the papers before anyone else did, as a way to divert suspicion away from herself.

And maybe Maribelle had been reading too many suspense novels lately.

Clem and Ginnie knew her better than that. They would never

suspect her, just as she would never suspect them … except that she'd had that brief moment of jaw-clenching doubt about Clem.

But it was crazy to think that either of the store's owners would steal from their own business.

That made even less sense than finding the tin of papers in the first place.

Or did it?

I definitely need to stop reading mysteries for a while, Maribelle thought to herself.

* * *

That afternoon, as Maribelle fretted over the mystery of the green tin, she decided she'd find herself a good children's book to take her mind off things when she got home this evening — maybe something with talking reindeer or singing Santas.

Oh, Santa!

She suddenly remembered that she still had some bad news to confess to Clem.

"Clem," Maribelle started, then the words stuck in her throat.

Her employer stopped what he was doing and looked up from the desk at her.

"Since I've already been the bearer of bad news today, I might as well get it *all* out." She hesitated, thinking maybe this wasn't such a good idea, after all. It could wait. But she'd already piqued Clem's curiosity, so she plunged ahead.

"I'm really, *really* sorry, Clem. I destroyed your ceramic Santa."

There. It was out.

"My ceramic Santa? Which one do you mean, dear?"

"The one from your childhood. The one your grandmother gave to your mother when she married your dad."

"You must be mistaken, Maribelle. I've never had a ceramic Santa," Clem said.

"What? I'm talking about the one we put out on display every Christmas from the top shelf of the storage closet."

"Nope. I don't think so," he said. "You must have dreamed that, young lady."

"But you told me about knocking him off the mantel with your wooden airplane when you were 7 years old. Remember? Your dad made you chop wood as punishment?"

"You must have read that in a book, my dear. Maybe that story you read to the children last year when I had laryngitis? I don't have a ceramic Santa, so if you broke one at the store, it had no sentimental value to me. In fact, I don't even like ceramic Santa Clauses, so there is no need for apologies. You can stop worrying."

He bent back over his task.

Maribelle needed to go to bed early tonight. Apparently the stress of being store manager was taking an even bigger toll on her than she realized.

As she walked out of the office to get back to work, she stepped on a shard of Santa Claus that she had missed with the broom.

5

By the time Joel left the hospital, he was feeling no pain.

The strong narcotic would wear off in a few hours, but for now, life was good. It was *goooood*.

Andre deposited him onto the front seat of his low-slung sports car — an endeavor that took longer than normal because of Joel's long legs and his state of medicated bliss — then went around and got in on the driver's side to start the engine. He used voice command to dial the office.

"Call 'Kim Office' on speakerphone," Andre told his vehicle.

While he waited for the phone to ring, he gathered his thoughts.

"Hey, Kim," Andre said to Kim's old-fashioned answering machine. "I'm taking Joel straight home. He's in no condition to work today. And he probably should take tomorrow off, too — that'll give him a three-day weekend to get back on his feet. Call me when you get this, and I'll fill you in."

Kandis, who was walking by Kim's office when the call came in, overheard Andre talking and rushed over to snatch up the receiver.

"Andre? It's Kandis. Is Joel OK?"

"He'll be fine. I gave Lizzie the details; have her fill you in. She's supposed to be getting a cleaning crew to take care of the broken glass. Do you know if she did?"

"Yeah, there's some woman named Ray in there right now. Do you know her?"

"She's legit," Andre assured her. "And Kandis? Whatever you do, do NOT try to make Elizabeth feel guilty about Joel's accident."

"Why would I?" Kandis said.

"For a couple of reasons," Andre replied. "One, she thinks it's her fault because he tripped over the golf clubs. I repeat: It's not her fault,

29

so don't try to lay a guilt trip on her. And, two, because of your jealousy of Lizzie and Joel's close relationship."

"Jealousy? I'm not jealous! Why would you think that?" Kandis asked Andre.

But she wasn't sure she wanted to hear the answer.

Andre glanced over at Joel, who appeared to be sleeping soundly, despite the noise from midday traffic and the conversation going on next to him. Nevertheless, Andre switched from the car speaker to his wireless headset just in case.

"Kandi, it's pretty obvious you have feelings for Joel that go beyond mere colleague status," he said gently.

"Oh," was all she could muster. Oh.

Then: "How many other people know?"

"Not many. Probably just me, Kim … and Elizabeth."

That's practically everyone!

"You don't think Joel suspects?" Again, she wasn't sure she wanted to know.

"Joel suspects that everyone loves him!" Andre laughed. "You know he's an optimist, that he loves most people and that he tries to keep his head down and his nose to the grindstone.

"And we're pretty close," Andre continued. "If he suspected, I would know."

"Why haven't you told him?" Kandis asked.

"Not my news to share, my friend."

"Thank you, Andre." Kandis felt relieved, but only a little. If half of their co-workers knew, what did that mean for the office? For her job? How long had they known? She wasn't even sure when *she* had realized she had feelings for him. How long before Joel would figure it out?

As if on cue, Joel raised his head and, without opening his eyes, shouted, "I love Kandi!" and went back to sleep.

6

As Joel arrived at work Monday morning, his cell phone rang.

"Unknown," his caller ID read.

He let it go to voicemail. Too many robocalls lately, the accountant thought as he locked the car door and headed for the office.

The minute he entered, three women practically tackled him.

Elizabeth was in the lead.

"JOEL!" she practically screamed.

"Oh, Joel, it's so good to see you! How's your arm?" his assistant asked.

"Better than it was last week; I'm a pretty quick healer. Plus, having a few days off — and pain medication — helped a lot, I think," he replied with a grin. "Except that I had some really strange dreams while I was medicated."

"Joel, I'm so sorry this happened. I …"

"Hey. No need for apologies. Accidents happen," Joel said. "My arm will be good as new in a week or two, and I'm happy to be back, happy to see you and the gang, and I'm ready to get to work."

"The gang" had to offer greetings and hugs — even an awkward attempt at a high-five — before Joel and Lizzie headed to his office to get him up to speed on what he had missed.

"Want some coffee?" Lizzie asked as they reached his door.

"I had two cups at home," Joel said as he opened the door and a nauseating scent nearly overwhelmed him.

"Whoa! Why does my office smell like that?"

"What are you smelling?" Lizzie asked.

"Well … it smells a lot like peppermint and … industrial cleaner?"

"OK, that makes sense. I just wondered if it was the peppermint you smelled, or the cleaner."

"Both," he said. "You know I don't care much for peppermint, so the combination of that and the other smell is almost too much."

"Oh, Joel! I forgot that you don't like peppermint! When the cleaning crew left after getting the blood out of your carpet, the scent was so strong I brought in my peppermint oil and diffuser to try to mask the smell. I came in early today to be sure I had the diffuser running before you got here."

"That was so thoughtful of you, Lizzie," Joel said quietly. He didn't want to make her feel bad, but the odor, combined with the fragile state of his stomach from the medications he had been taking, threatened to nauseate him to the point that he couldn't stay in his office.

"Joel, what can I do?" his assistant asked.

"Well, we can't open the windows; it's way too cold outside. I may just have to work in the conference room today, and we could crack the office windows a little when we head home this evening; maybe the scent will be gone when we get back tomorrow."

He and Lizzie gathered his laptop and a few office supplies from the desk and headed for the large room down the hall.

Kandis, who had not been part of the welcoming committee when Joel arrived at work, was already sitting at the conference table, papers spread all around.

"Oh, hi, Kandis," Joel said. "I didn't realize anyone was using the room."

"Joel!" Kandis said, knocking her coffee cup over onto one of the paper piles.

Joel and Lizzie rushed to help, each grabbing a bunch of papers and heading for the marble-topped credenza at one end of the room.

The conference room occasionally doubled as a dining room when the agency had all-day meetings with clients, and they kept a stash of white linen napkins in one of the drawers.

"These aren't very absorbent, but they'll have to do until we can get some paper towels," Joel said. Lizzie hurried to the break room and brought back a roll. She started sopping up the dark liquid as Joel and Kandis blotted printouts.

"Kandis, I'm sorry we startled you, but why are you in here instead of your office?" Joel asked. "Don't tell me yours smells like industrial cleaner, too."

"No, my office smells fine," Kandis replied. "It's just that this audit is fairly complicated, and there wasn't room on my desk to spread out like I needed to. There's something not quite right that I haven't been able to put my finger on, and I thought I could sort things into categories that might help me figure it out."

"Maybe I could help you," Joel said as he continued to blot papers. "I need to work in here until my office airs out — unless I would disturb you."

"No!" Kandis blurted.

Joel raised his eyebrows, and Kandis paused her blotting as she asked herself why she had reacted the way she did.

Did she say that because she didn't want him in here ... or because she did?

He definitely would be distracting, but that didn't mean she didn't want him there. The distraction was totally because it was Joel. If anyone else were sharing the room with her, she could focus on her work and ignore just about anything.

But Joel was a completely different story.

7

Something seemed to be making Kandis edgy, Joel thought after Lizzie had left them alone in the conference room.

They had salvaged most of the coffee-stained work, and what couldn't be salvaged she'd had Terrance reprint and stack neatly in piles, as they originally had been. But that didn't seem to calm her down.

She seemed to have a nervous energy, fumbling with papers, talking faster than usual.

"Kandis, is something wrong?" Joel asked. "Do you need help getting the new printouts organized?"

"No, it's not that," Kandis said.

"Then what? What's got you so distracted? I can help you go over the spreadsheets and reports for your audit. I told you I'd help."

"It's not the audit, Joel."

He waited for her to continue, but she didn't. She just stared at the stacks of printouts, looking conflicted — refusing to make eye contact.

"Kandi, talk to me. I think we're close enough that you know you can trust me, and you know I can hold a confidence."

"Yes, I know that, Joel, and it's one of my favorite things about you — your trustworthiness."

Joel went around the conference table and sat in the chair next to Kandis. He put his hand over hers, sending a tingle up her spine.

She took her hand away, a move that Joel misinterpreted, and he immediately apologized.

"No, Joel, it's OK," she assured him. "You didn't do anything wrong."

She had removed her hand from his because it made it harder to speak. An internal conflict was raging — should she bring it up, or should she wait for him to? But she was brave, she reminded herself. She would be the first to speak about their feelings for each other. She needed a moment to muster the courage, however.

"Joel ..."

Still, he waited.

"Whatever it is, it can't be as bad as all that. Tell me, Kandis," he said gently.

Ever since Joel had entered the conference room, she had been trying to read him. She'd seen nothing in his demeanor to suggest that the feelings he had declared last week — granted, when he was heavily medicated — were on his mind today.

But she was tired of this internal war. Even if she had misinterpreted his feelings, she had to get it out there so she could put it to rest and get on with her life — preferably with Joel, but moving on, no matter the response.

"This is difficult to talk about, especially with you sitting there looking at me," Kandis said. (*Especially with the purple of your sweater playing up your beautiful green eyes.*) "But even if you hate me when you hear how I feel, I can't go on wondering."

"I could never hate you, Kandis," Joel said, the gentleness still in his voice. "I can tell that whatever it is, it's torturing you. I won't judge you, no matter what you tell me. Just say it."

"OK," she said, her heart rate increasing by the second. "Last week, when Andre was driving you home from the hospital, you said, 'I love Kandi.' I know you were under the influence of medication, but often things like that bring out the truth. ...

"Tell me the truth, Joel. Did you mean it?"

"Did I mean ..."

"That you ..." The words stuck in her throat.

Come on, girl. You're being brave today, remember?

"That you love me."

There. It was out.

She wanted to die. All at once, her doubts came rushing back. Maybe she misinterpreted. Maybe she misheard. Maybe it was all a dream ... a nightmare, if she was wrong.

For a moment, Joel was speechless. It took him a few seconds to absorb what Kandis had just said. How had she gotten the impression that he had romantic feelings for her? What did she mean, he said "I love Kandi"? He didn't remember saying that. But she was right: He was pretty medicated when he and Andre left the emergency room. But still ... why would he say something like that when it wasn't true?

But slowly it dawned on him:

He remembered having a dream — or more like a hallucination — while Andre drove him home. He heard Andre say something about candy, and in his mind they were driving through a strange land full of swirly, twirly gumdrops, lollipops and cotton candy, in something like Munchkinland from *The Wizard of Oz*. He remembered waking up at home with a massive sugar craving.

So maybe he did say he loved … *candy.*

That's right. He remembered. He said he loved candy.

The thought crushed him. He knew Kandis would be hurt and embarrassed when she found out her error. He wasn't sure how to break it to his friend. He knew she was lonely — fragile, even — and he didn't want to wound her even further. But he also didn't want to give her the false impression that he had romantic feelings for her. Best to let her know right away.

He put his hand on her arm.

"Kandi …"

Immediately, she knew she had been mistaken. One look into Joel's eyes confirmed her fear that it had all been just a dream. Not Joel's dream, but hers. What a fool for thinking he felt the same way she did. How on earth had she convinced herself that he could ever love her?

Oh, who was she trying to kid? She knew exactly how she had convinced herself. She'd had feelings for Joel for so long that she had grasped at the tiniest sliver of hope, even when she knew that she was grasping, clawing, for his affection.

He didn't love her.

She wasn't worthy of love. Of course he didn't return her feelings. She was incapable of being the type of person a man like Joel could care for.

"Joel, don't say it. I already know: I was stupid for assuming you were speaking your mind lucidly last week. How could you love me? I'm not lovable." A tear slid down Kandis' cheek.

"No!" Joel scolded her. "Don't ever say that. I believe that God made each of us as a unique creature, and we have worth because he created us in his image. And beyond that, even if I didn't believe that about God and his love for us, I would believe that you are immeasurably lovable."

"Joel, how can you say that? I've never been in a relationship that lasted. I'm too needy, too clingy … even desperate, if I'm being honest. It's no wonder a man doesn't want to be with me past the second or third date.

"It's why I gave up. I became a coward. I put a wall up. You know that about me, Joel. I hold everyone — even the people closest to me — at arm's length. No one wants to be with me."

"Totally untrue, my friend," Joel said. "For starters, if you were a coward, you never would have talked to me about your feelings."

"Well, technically, I was talking about *your* feelings," Kandis reminded him.

He laughed.

"True. But if we're being strictly technical, you were brave enough to bring up the subject, even if I did have to do a little coaxing. If you were that cowardly, you wouldn't have talked to me about it, no matter how I tried to persuade you to."

That made the corners of her mouth turn up, if only slightly.

"You're just saying that to make me feel better," she said.

"Did it work?" he asked.

"A little."

"Kandis, you are an incredible woman. You're smart, funny, beautiful, hardworking … and brave."

"If I'm all those things, Joel, then why don't you want me? What's missing?"

"Kandis, you know about my faith in God. You know that I follow Jesus and try to do everything according to his leading, right?"

"Yes. I don't understand it, but I know it's true."

"Well, maybe what I'm about to say won't make sense to you. Maybe it won't make you feel better, but I hope you understand when I say that I believe God has a special woman designed just for me ... and, as much as I care for you and our friendship, I know I'm still waiting for the right one. I haven't met her yet."

Another tear fell from Kandis' cheek.

"I think you're a fantastic person, Kandi, even if you don't recognize your own wonderful qualities," Joel said. "On paper, we'd probably come close to making a great match. It's not that at all.

"It's just that … well, when I meet the woman I'm supposed to spend my life with, she needs to believe in Jesus, too. So, in answer to your question about what's missing: It's faith."

"Oh," was all that Kandis could say.

"When I was in high school, I dated a girl who didn't believe in God. We had a lot of interests in common, but what initially attracted me was her intellect; she was super-smart, witty and confident. We dated for a few months, but I never had a sense of peace about it. I knew what the Bible said about being 'unequally yoked,' but I had ignored it because I was so attracted to this girl.

"Eventually, I couldn't bear my conscience — my disobedience — any longer. I broke up with her, even though it tore me apart to do it. I was in love with her, after all. The thing is, Kandis, I'd rather be in a right relationship with God than to be in a relationship with a person I know is not his best choice for me."

"Why is it so important that you both believe in God?" Kandis asked.

"For so many reasons, Kandi," Joel said. "For starters, because he told us to in his Word, the Bible. It's an act of obedience, and if it's nothing else — if I lived my entire life without understanding why he said it should be this way — that would be reason enough."

"I don't get it," Kandis said. "How could you accept that just because he said so?"

"Because I trust Him."

She raised her eyebrows, and Joel wasn't sure whether she was surprised to hear his answer, she was challenging him, or exactly what was going through her mind. But she seemed willing to listen, so he continued.

"I trust God because I know him. I grew up hearing about him, reading his word and getting to know him. I know he's good, and he has a perfect plan for our lives. His plans are *always* for our good, even when we don't necessarily like or understand what he has in mind for us. Sometimes our circumstances are hard, and he allows that for various reasons.

"Sometimes it's because we've disobeyed God — in other words, we've sinned. Not always, but sometimes. Sometimes our tough position is the result of bad choices we've made, and we're suffering the natural consequences of our choices — or someone else's bad choices."

Kandis shifted in her chair.

"Go on," she said.

"It may sound harsh to think that God allows us to suffer because of someone else's bad choices, but we see that all around us every day. The world is falling apart in so many ways. It was never meant to be this way, but God allows his creatures — humans — choices in the way we live our lives. Sometimes those choices are really stupid and selfish, and those selfish choices can have devastating results.

"I know we were talking about relationships and romantic love," Joel said, "but our sin and rebellion toward God play out in every area of life. Because we're in a fallen world — a world of broken relationships and systems and governments, of natural disasters and manmade disasters, of hatred and wars and crime — it's crucial that we stay as close to God as possible, that we follow his leading and do our best to obey his will for us."

He paused.

"Is any of this making sense?" Joel asked Kandis. "Because there is a point to what I'm trying to explain."

"Sort of," Kandis said. "I see that you'd want God on your side with all the craziness in the world."

"Yes, but even more than trying to please Him so he'll be 'on my side,' so to speak, I want to please Him because I love Him. God sacrificed so much for me — for the whole world — that my response should always be to love Him and do my best to obey."

"What do you mean he sacrificed so much for you, and the world?" Kandis asked. "It seems like we're the ones doing all the sacrificing."

"Yeah, I get that. When I'm really stressed out or lonely or angry about something that has happened in the world — especially if it has a direct effect on me — I tend to think I'm sacrificing an awful lot by living my life for God. Sometimes I think, 'What difference does it make if I'm good? The world's just a rotten, stinkin' place, and it's always going to be a rotten, stinkin' place,' " Joel laughed.

"That's what I was thinking." Kandis laughed for the first time since Joel had entered the conference room.

"My third-grade Sunday school teacher used to call that stinkin' thinkin', " Joel said. "I hated it back then, but that woman taught me a lot about being a godly man. So did my parents."

"So this sacrificing business," Kandis reminded him. "Why do you say that HE sacrificed for the world?"

"What do you know about Jesus?" Joel asked.

"Well, unlike you, I did *not* go to Sunday school, but I know that Jesus was a philosopher who claimed to be God, and I know that he died on a cross and his followers claimed that he rose from the dead."

"I believe that Jesus was more than just a philosopher, a teacher or 'a good man,' as some people describe him," Joel said. "And I believe that he *did* rise from the dead. There's plenty of evidence that says he did."

"OK, just for the sake of argument, let's say that's all true," Kandis said. "How does that relate to what you said about sacrifice?"

"When Jesus died … wait, let me back up a minute.

"Do you believe that humans are intrinsically good, or bad?" Joel asked Kandis.

"From what I've observed, most of us are pretty self-centered," she said.

"That's not just your observation, my friend. That's God's conclusion, as well. And he said we're *all* self-centered. Not a single one of us is righteous on our own merit. He made mankind in his own image, but he also gave us free will. That means we're free to do right … or do wrong. Too often we do wrong.

"Because God is holy, and because we've fallen short of his standard of holiness and can't possibly make up for it, no matter how hard we try, he had to provide a way out.

"You see, God isn't merely a God of love. He's a God of justice. We've fallen short of his standard, and there's no way we could stand before him on Judgment Day and even hope to measure up. So he had to provide a substitute. That substitute — the sacrifice we were talking about — was Jesus Christ."

"I need a drink of water," Kandis said, rising from her chair. Joel could see that she had started to perspire, despite how cool the conference room was this morning.

"Am I overwhelming you with all this?" he asked.

"Maybe a little. It's a lot to think about."

"Would it help if I told you the story has a happy ending?"

"I could use one of those right about now," she said. "But maybe you could tell me about it later. I really need to get back to the audit. Do you still want to help me?"

"Of course."

As Kandis headed for the break room for a glass of water, Joel was disappointed that they didn't get to finish their conversation, but he was encouraged that she hadn't closed the door on it. He planned to do some praying about Part 2 of their talk. He would ask the Lord to provide another opportunity soon, that he would give Joel the right words and that Kandis would open her heart to Jesus.

8

Joel had dropped the subject of God after speaking so openly to Kandis about his faith and the reasons they couldn't be together. He prayed that another opportunity would present itself soon.

But he asked himself if Kandis' lack of faith was the only reason he hadn't wanted a relationship with her, and he had to admit that it was more than that. It wasn't just that God hadn't led him to care for her in that way; mismatched couples get together all the time outside of God's will (although they often claim that he made them for each other).

No, Joel had never felt a spark of interest in Kandis, even before he knew that she lacked faith in Jesus, and he sensed that he wouldn't want a romantic relationship with her even if she became a Christian. Friendship, of course; the Lord had given him a love for people in general, and Joel had many friends. Love and marriage? Probably not. He wasn't ruling anything out, but Kandis just didn't seem to be "the one."

Much of the time lately, he had been waffling between wanting to be a bachelor for the rest of his life and desiring to meet a special woman — *the* woman — God had designed to be his lifelong mate. Sometimes those thoughts battled for prime real estate in his brain. One minute he convinced himself he would stay single forever; the next minute the longing in his heart to find a wonderful young lady and settle down nearly knocked him to his knees. He knew that not everyone's story ended up like his parents' had. That situation hadn't had a happy ending, but Joel still believed, deep down, that God had a special lady in mind just for him, and he was willing to wait for her, no matter how long it took.

Sometimes "willing to wait," though, showed up as fear, disguised as paralysis, wrapped up in a tightly woven blanket of angst. It wasn't pretty when his heart went to that place.

Partly because of the fear and angst, Joel hadn't been pursuing anyone, and one of his Christian buddies had told him recently, "You've gotta get out there, man. God ain't gonna just drop a chick in your lap."

"Well, he might," Joel joked. "You never know; the Lord works in mysterious ways."

"Dude, you know I'm right," the friend had said. "Remember that joke about the guy sitting on his roof after the town flooded? When he got to heaven — after he *drowned*, dude — he wondered why God didn't save him. God said to him, 'I sent two boats and a helicopter. What more did you need?' *Right*?"

Yes, Joel knew his buddy was right. "The Lord helps those who help themselves" isn't exactly in the Bible, but he couldn't expect God to just drop a woman into his lap, as his friend had so eloquently pointed out.

He needed to be a little proactive.

It wasn't like he was planning to change his aftershave and start bar hopping. Nope, that wasn't his style. He guessed he just needed to start paying closer attention to the world — and the women — around him. Maybe respond a little more openly to them.

For far too long, Joel had hidden behind the wall of busyness that came with his job. It's not as though he needed the extra income; he had a good retirement account, plenty in savings and the nice little house he had bought a few years after college. At 35, he had all the accoutrements of success, as the world defined success.

Except for a companion.

And that didn't count his bulldog, Shirley.

Granted, Shirley was a great companion — loyal, dependable, not loud or too messy, as a lot of dogs are, able to be left alone for long stretches — but canine companionship goes only so far.

Yes, Joel definitely needed to put some effort into meeting Ms. Right.

Trouble was, the only places he went were work, church and the grocery store.

Dating a co-worker was out of the question. Too awkward. In fact, he hoped his recent conversation with Kandis didn't make work relations awkward between the two of them. Whether they dated successfully or eventually broke up, he just didn't see romantic relationships between co-workers as a good idea, especially in a small company like Goldman & Blackburn Accounting. He had seen it go both ways with friends and acquaintances, and even when the couples worked out, there could be tension at the office.

The church he attended was on the small side, too, and the pickings were slim. Only a handful of the women his age were single, and most of them seemed to be so focused on their careers or other concerns that they didn't have time for dating. One was trying to run a new business, and she put in more hours at the office than he did at his job; another seemed to be trying to climb the corporate ladder, and she used every opportunity to network with those farther along in their careers. One was fresh from a divorce and trying to make sure her children were taken care of. He stopped there. No sense in continuing to enumerate all the women who weren't interested in him or in whom he wasn't interested.

That left the grocery store.

And, with that thought, he decided he'd better put his nose to the grindstone and see how much catching up he needed to do on his work after being out for the past few days.

As if on cue, his phone rang.

Another "unknown" on the caller ID. He pushed "decline," but he noticed that he had a voicemail, presumably from the call he had ignored when he was arriving at work that morning. Before he could check it, another voicemail notification appeared.

Both messages were from the same person: a man identifying himself as Clement Hatch from Bedford Books on the other side of town. He said he knew Joel's father, and Dad had given him Joel's number. He needed to talk to Joel about a confidential matter, and it was urgent.

Clement had left his cell phone number instead of the bookstore's number. Until they'd had a preliminary meeting, he didn't want anyone besides Ginnie to know that he was calling in a CPA to audit their books.

Joel hit the callback button on his cell, and Clem answered immediately.

"Mr. Hatch? This is Joel Stewart returning your call."

"Oh, thank goodness, Joel. Thank you for calling me back."

"What can I do for you, Mr. Hatch? You sounded pretty desperate."

"I'm sorry to bother you — and to sound desperate — but we sort of are. We have a situation at the bookstore that my wife and I own. In fact, it's where we met you when you were a little boy. Do you remember?"

"Bedford Books … hmm, I do remember going there a few times many years ago. Were you the man who read stories to the kids and handed out hot chocolate and candy canes at Christmastime?"

"That was me!" Clem said proudly.

"Yes, I remember! I always thought you were a very nice man, Mr. Hatch."

"Call me Clem," the older gentleman said.

"So where would you like to meet?"

9

Maribelle had never won any awards for being graceful. In fact, she was so klutzy that a high school friend used to call her Gracie as a joke. It stung, but she got used to it. Sort of.

It seemed that no matter how sensible the shoes Maribelle wore (flat and boring most of the time), how clear the path she walked on, or how much heed she paid to her surroundings, she was simply destined to stumble and tumble through life.

So it should have come as no surprise when, barely halfway through the office door the morning after Clem's phone call to Joel, Maribelle's foot became entangled in a string of Christmas lights on the floor, causing her to lose her balance so completely that she fell sideways into Clem's green leather office chair.

But Clem's green leather office chair already held an occupant.

When Maribelle made a fool of herself, she was an expert at it. At home, she usually tripped over something small where the only witness was Dickens, and he would never tell. No, here at the bookstore she had to fall hard — and into the arms of a handsome, dark-haired stranger with piercing green eyes.

"Oh!" Maribelle exclaimed. "I'm so sorry!"

To regain her balance, she tried to put one hand on the edge of the desk to push herself off, but she missed. That only landed her squarely on Joel's lap ... and into his arms. He groaned and touched his right arm gingerly, feeling for fresh blood where the recent wound had been sutured.

Maribelle scrambled to her feet, but not before noticing that Joel's legs were long and muscular. So were the arms that helped steady her as she stood. Joel gave no indication that she had hurt his injured arm. He merely helped her to stand upright, then stood and looked at her.

If she hadn't been so flustered, the pretty manager might have thought it odd that a strange man had been sitting in Bedford Books' private office, occupying Clem's chair like it belonged to him.

Now, standing several inches taller than Maribelle, Joel Stewart seemed to be saying something to her.

"I'm sorry, what did you say?"

"I said, 'Are you all right?' It looked like you twisted your ankle when you lost your balance."

"No, no, I'm fine," Maribelle assured him, willing herself not to blush, which, of course, made her fair skin even pinker. "Nothing wounded but my pride, and that's been wounded more times than I can count."

"Oh, good, good." That was all Joel could think of to say. He was busy trying not to look too intently into Maribelle's pale blue eyes, but he found it difficult. Her curly, strawberry-blond hair, though now disheveled, was enchanting. It actually smelled sweetly of strawberry shampoo.

All Maribelle could think was, *Wow, he sure fills out that purple turtleneck nicely. And he's nice and tall.*

"So ... who are you, and what are you doing in Clem's office?" she said, working to recover her wits and trying to act like a mature adult — a bookstore manager, not a seventh-grade girl.

"Uh, I'm Joel Stewart, a friend of the Hatches'. Well, sort of. My dad, who was a friend of Clem's, used to bring me to the bookstore when I was a boy, and Clem was always really nice to me. We hadn't seen each other in years, but he called me yesterday to say he needed a favor, and I was between jobs, so I came right over."

"What kind of favor?" Maribelle knew she was being nosy, but she wondered whether Joel's sudden appearance had anything to do with the green tin of unpaid bills she had found. After all, Joel was sitting at Clem's desk, in Clem's chair.

She was a little protective of the items in and on that desk. And, as bookstore manager, she felt she had a right to know why a stranger had taken up court in her office. Well ... Clem and Ginnie's office.

"I'm a CPA," Joel said. "Clem wanted me to take a look at the books. I'm surprised he didn't tell you he had called me. I assume you're Maribelle?"

It was less a question than a statement.

"Yes," she said. "I'm the store manager, and I'm surprised, too. Why wouldn't he tell me? And exactly what did he ask you to do?" She knew they needed some outside counsel, but she hadn't expected

Clem to invite someone in so quickly ... or so *not-ancient*. And attractive.

"He said you had found a hidden stash of unpaid bills and that some of your vendors were complaining that your accounts were past due. He wanted me to take a look to see if I could tell what was going on. He doesn't want any of the other employees to know I'm doing this. That's why I came so early in the morning. But I thought he had planned to tell you."

"Is Clem here?" She hadn't even had a chance to take off her coat. Clem and Ginnie had started coming in much later, so this whole situation seemed odd. Then again, the whole situation *was* odd.

"Ginnie's here, but she said Clem wasn't feeling well today, so he won't be in — at least until afternoon, if at all. They want me to be gone by 7:45, so she and I got here at 6:30. So far I haven't had much chance to do anything but look over the invoices that were hidden in the desk drawer. I was waiting for you to arrive so I could ask you to show me your electronic bookkeeping system. What kind of software do you use for that? Clem wasn't sure."

Maribelle couldn't decide whether to be embarrassed or proud when she told Joel, "I just use spreadsheets. When I took over the books from Clem a few months ago, I took an online course and converted what he had been doing on paper to my own electronic version of his ledger. So far it's worked ... or at least I thought it was working. Now I'm not so sure."

"May I see the spreadsheets you've been using?" Joel asked softly.

Maribelle got a knot in her stomach and suddenly started doubting her competence and imagining all kinds of scenarios. What if she had been doing it all wrong? What if Joel found errors that confirmed that Maribelle didn't have a clue what she was doing when it came to managing the store's finances? (Did she?) What if the errors pointed to her, making it seem as though she had been the one to hide the bills in the green tin?

This was not the first time the thought had occurred to Maribelle that people might suspect her of hiding the bills and neglecting to pay the vendors.

But the whole thing just didn't make any sense. Why were only certain bills left unpaid? Why were the electricity and water bills not included in the hidden stash? Maybe the thief (as she had started referring to the culprit in her head) was afraid that would arouse suspicion. After all, if the utility bills went unpaid, they'd all be sitting in the dark. No customers, no Christmas lights (to trip over), no heat, no water for peppermint tea … in other words, total disaster.

Speaking of peppermint tea, the urge to have a cup nearly overwhelmed her.

"Before I show you the spreadsheets, would you mind if I fixed myself a cup of tea? It usually relaxes me, and I can tell you, this whole mess has kept me awake at night. I could use a nice cup of tea right now."

"No, go ahead. I'll wait."

Maribelle had to squeeze past Joel, who had sat back down in Clem's chair while they talked, to open the desk drawer for her tea tin. As she bent down, a whiff of Joel's aftershave nearly made her lose her balance again.

Holy moly, she thought. *Why does he have to smell so good? For now, this guy is the enemy. I can't let myself get caught up in his dreamy green eyes or his long legs or his …*

Incredible-smelling cologne.

When she opened the tin of tea, Joel got a strong whiff of peppermint.

Ugh, he thought. *Why did it have to be peppermint? I hope the smell doesn't overtake the room while she's drinking it. Is there a window we could open? Maybe she'll slug it down fast.*

Maribelle took out a tea bag and told Joel she'd be right back.

Before she grabbed her mug from the break room, she went to find Ginnie.

"Oh, Maribelle," Ginnie said. "I'm sorry I was busy when you got here. I was talking to my sister, who's in Europe right now. She called just before you got here. But I just overheard you talking to Joel, so I guess I don't need to introduce you."

"No, but I came out here to make sure he was legit. He said he's a CPA and that Clem hired him."

"Well, I don't know if you could say we hired him, dear. Right now he's just doing us a favor. He refused to let us pay him until he makes some preliminary observations to see if he can determine what's going on. But I have a feeling we're going to be keeping him around for a few days."

"He said you don't want any of the employees to know he's here, and I think that's wise," Maribelle said. "But how is he going to examine the books if he's not here?"

"I'm going to let him take the tin of invoices with him, and I was hoping you would have a way for him to look at your electronic bookkeeping system offsite, as well."

"I suppose I could email him the spreadsheets. I would need to spend a few minutes looking at them first, though," Maribelle said. "I have the store's accounting system in the same workbook as some other files that he won't need to examine. I'll need to separate them out."

"Whatever you need to do, dear. Just give Joel whatever he asks for. We trust him implicitly. We've known his family for years, and when we called his accounting firm, the owner said there was no one more trustworthy than Joel Stewart."

"OK, Ginnie. I'll work with him on the spreadsheets — after I fix my tea! By the way, he mentioned that Clem is sick today. Not too serious, I hope."

"He just wasn't quite feeling himself. I think he just needs a day off. This invoice situation has got him pacing the floors and staying awake at night. We need to get to the bottom of this soon."

"I agree," Maribelle said. "I'll go fix my tea so we can get Joel out of here before the others start arriving."

And before I become intoxicated by the scent of his aftershave, she muttered under her breath.

✳ ✳ ✳

"What are you looking for?" Maribelle asked Joel as she logged on to take a look at the computer files before turning them over to Joel. "I mean, how do you tell when someone's been messing with the numbers?"

"First, I'll take the bills you found in the metal tin and compare them to the spreadsheets and the bank statements. By the way, when did you start using the spreadsheets? In other words, how far back do the electronic files go versus the paper versions that Clem used to keep?"

"I took over as store manager at the beginning of the year. It took me about two weeks to transfer everything from the handwritten paper documents to the software after I took the online course to learn how to actually use the spreadsheets. I spent two or three days taking the course because I repeated some of the lessons a couple of times. I think I got a pretty good handle on how to do it, but I recognize that I still have a lot to learn when it comes to spreadsheets and bookkeeping.

"I mean, I've always been pretty good at numbers, but I figured it'd be better to have everything in a system that could calculate the numbers for me," Maribelle babbled, barely taking a breath. "At first I had to double-check the calculations because I just didn't trust the program to do it correctly — after all, I was new to this whole computerized-spreadsheet business — but eventually I felt more comfortable trusting the system. Obviously I didn't trust it enough, because look what has happened."

Maribelle paused to breathe.

Why am I going on and on about spreadsheets and calculations? she asked herself. *And why did I have to say "look what has happened," like this whole mess is my fault? All he asked was how long the store has been using the electronic bookkeeping method.*

Apparently Joel made her nervous. Was that because she was afraid she had screwed up the store's accounting system or because he was so incredibly good looking? *Distractingly good looking.*

She supposed it didn't matter. If it was the former, that could be fixed. Maybe he could even show her where she went wrong, once he figured out what actually *was* wrong. And if it was the latter, well, that was totally irrelevant. She didn't need to be getting all moon-eyed over some accountant. Especially one who was so obviously …

Good looking.

He really was good looking.

Those green eyes …

STOP IT, MARIBELLE! Just … stop it.

And he smelled wonderful.

Sigh. She was hopeless.

She took a long swig of tea, nearly choking on it, and told herself to snap out of it.

Besides, she realized that Joel had never finished answering her question about what he was looking for in the store's records. She wondered whether that was deliberate.

Was he trying to evade the question? Did he suspect her? What if he did? What if all the clues led to her?

Well, he would figure out that she had nothing to do with it, even if she hadn't necessarily been competent with the spreadsheets.

Right?

Her imagination was out of control, and she needed to get a grip.

She reached for another tea bag.

10

Maribelle returned to the office with her second cup of peppermint tea, and Joel tried to hold his breath. He knew that effort wouldn't last long — he had to breathe, after all — but it was either that or leave the room until she finished her tea, and he wanted to keep a careful eye on what Maribelle was about to do on the computer.

Despite Clem and Ginnie's trust in Maribelle — and despite the fact that his instincts told him she wasn't to blame — Joel wasn't ruling anything out as he looked into the store's financial situation. He would keep an open mind because he knew that making assumptions could cause him to overlook something crucial. That mindset went against his natural state of optimism, but he had been an accountant for too long to take any piece of information for granted.

A few years earlier, he had watched a documentary about a city treasurer who bilked her municipality out of more than $50 million, and no one suspected a thing for the longest time. When the official's crimes were brought to light, however, it was revealed that auditors and bankers had acted negligently in regard to this municipal employee, who had been entrusted with her city's tax dollars. Those auditors and bankers were called to account — literally and figuratively — in the court system, and the city subsequently made several structural changes in its leadership and in the oversight of those public officials.

Joel didn't want to be cynical (even though he had gradually become so in many ways), but stories like that helped him to realize that he needed to be diligent and not let outward appearances, assumptions or his usually reliable intuition cause him to neglect his duties to keep people's money — their livelihoods — safe.

He felt that the Lord had given him stewardship over a certain segment of the population: those who entrusted their financial affairs to Goldman & Blackburn, and even friends who sought him out for advice. The weight of his responsibility was sometimes heavy, and he prayed that the case of Bedford Books would turn out to be just some sort of weird misunderstanding.

Not likely, but he could hope. He liked the Hatches, for some odd reason he felt drawn to Maribelle, and he wanted this to turn out well for the couple and all of the store's trusted employees — they seemed to be like family to one another. But he needed to proceed with as much impartiality as possible.

He watched Maribelle boot up the computer, open a folder labeled Accounting and double-click a file called Bills and Financial Reports.

She acted a little nervous as she opened the spreadsheet, but maybe it was just because someone was looking over her shoulder. That threw people off sometimes. Nevertheless, because his training and experience had taught him not to assume anything, he kept watching.

"I need to delete a couple of spreadsheets before I show you the entire contents of the folder," Maribelle said softly.

Joel leaned in a little closer. "Could you repeat that? I didn't catch it all."

She repeated her statement a little more loudly, although with no less reluctance.

"I'd like to see what those spreadsheets contain, if you don't mind."

Maribelle took a deep breath and said, "Well, it's kind of embarrassing."

"Ms. Reed, I understand, but your employers have asked me to help them determine what's going on with their financials, and I need to see everything. They've given me permission to dig in as deeply as I need to. You can trust me not to reveal embarrassing personal secrets about you, but I'm going to have to see what you intend to delete."

He had seen so many crazy things in people's financial records over the years, it would take a lot to surprise him.

"It's not exactly a *personal secret*," she emphasized. "Although I guess having this conversation is making it seem so."

She sat there for several seconds, took a few sips of her tea, then took a deep breath and let it out slowly.

Joel turned his head just enough to avoid the aroma of peppermint but not enough to take his eyes off the computer file.

He waited.

Maribelle picked up her teacup, swirled it around and took a few more sips — actually more like gulps — while Joel held his breath.

Finish your tea, lady, Joel thought, trying not to become impatient. But enough was enough.

"So ... are you gonna let me see what's in those files?" he asked gently. He didn't want to make her uncomfortable, but c'mon. This was getting ridiculous.

"OK, first let me just give you some background. I've always wanted to be a novelist, like Louisa May Alcott or Jane Austen or the Bronte sisters. Or maybe ... well, that's beside the point," Maribelle said, reining in the compulsion to start babbling again. "Except it's not. Because ... well, I also read a lot of contemporary romance novels. They say you're supposed to study the type of books you want to write. I'm still trying to figure that out — exactly what type of books I might be able to be successful at and enjoy writing — so I read a lot of books written by women. Some are old, some much newer."

She paused to catch her breath, because she had started talking pretty fast, despite her efforts to calm herself. Now that she was revealing her secret, she wanted to get it over with. But she always over-explained when she got nervous.

She took another sip of tea.

Joel held his breath.

She put the cup down and continued.

"I don't have a computer at home. Well, I did, but it crashed and I haven't been able to afford to replace it. I plan to, but in the meantime, I started keeping a record of all the books I've read — romances and other things that I didn't want people to know I was reading — on the computer here. Only I didn't want anyone to find my list, so I hid it in the financial records because I'm the only one who uses those files.

"I know it sounds crazy — why would I be embarrassed for anyone to know I read romance novels, after all — but it's just that, well, I have kind of a reputation around here for being ... hmm ... well, let's just say somewhat jaded or cynical. I've sort of looked down my nose at people who buy romances from Bedford Books, like they should be reading something more ... serious. More *substantive*."

Joel leaned his elbow on the desk and rested his chin on his hand. He let her talk.

"Only now that I've started reading some of them, I realize that they're not all like I thought they were. I really like some of them. But I don't even buy my romance novels at Bedford Books, which is crazy on *so many* levels. But there's my reputation to uphold, and all that. Crow is not exactly my favorite dish."

She had been talking a mile a minute again, but now she was

finished. Probably.

Whew! She thought. *Her secret was out, and he hadn't laughed.*

She sat back in her chair, swished around her now-tepid tea, and drained the cup.

Whew! Joel thought. *That's the end of the tea!*

11

When Maribelle finally arrived home that night, all she wanted to do was curl up with her cat, a good book and a steaming cup of peppermint tea.

She knew Dickens would love that idea, too. As soon as he heard Maribelle turn her key in the lock, he leapt from his window perch and ran to the door. Once inside, the exhausted bookstore manager was greeted with loud purring and the warmth of her cat's body pressing against her legs. Before Maribelle could hang her coat on the rack just inside the door, he had weaved in and out three times, covering the bottom of her green tights with gray cat hair.

"I need to brush you, Dickens. Looks like Laney hasn't done that this week; has she been feeding you your lunch on time?" *MEOW.* "I'll have to check in with her."

Dickens loved to be pampered and fussed over, and the mere mention of the word *brush* sent him in delirious circles around Maribelle, his purr-engine kicking into overdrive. When he was convinced she understood that the brushing needed to happen *now* — before dinner, before peppermint tea — he stopped circling and ran to the shelf where she kept his grooming tools.

Maribelle followed, after kicking off her flats by the door, and discovered that Dickens' brush wasn't in its usual place. She looked around the apartment for it, Dickens helping her search under furniture and cabinetry, but it was nowhere to be seen.

Finally she looked eye to eye with her old gray rescue cat and said, "Well, my friend, I guess we'll have to skip it until I can ask Laney what she's done with your brush."

The young woman across the hall had been coming in each weekday for the past few months to feed Dickens his lunch. Maribelle had asked her to brush him at least once a week, too — and more often, if she had time. Laney had college classes at night, and Maribelle knew she wouldn't be home right now. But with Dickens glaring at her, she decided to take a chance on texting Laney. Maybe she'd see the message and be able to reply discreetly. It was worth a shot. Better than having Dickens give her the kitty cold-shoulder the entire rest of the evening.

Maribelle: Laney do you know where D's brush is?

While the buddies waited for a response, Maribelle decided to change into a comfy sweatshirt and stretch pants and see what was in the freezer.

After giving Dickens a kitty treat that she hoped would appease him, then reheating and devouring a serving of leftovers on the verge of freezer burn, Maribelle put the kettle on for tea and grabbed her book — a cozy mystery — from the nightstand.

This book was one she wasn't embarrassed to be seen reading, so it was a physical book, not one she had downloaded to her password-protected e-reader.

As she picked up the afghan at the end of the sofa and sat down where they could watch the snow falling softly just outside their small window, she invited Dickens to come up before placing the afghan over her legs.

Still, the kitty stink-eye.

Sigh.

She looked at her phone to be sure she hadn't missed a reply from Laney and realized she had a text message from an unknown number.

"Hi, Ms. Reed. This is Joel Stewart. I'm sorry to bother you this evening, but I've been looking over your spreadsheets and have a few more questions for you. Will you be in the bookstore at 7 a.m. tomorrow?"

Great, Maribelle thought. *I was going to spend the evening trying to put the stupid spreadsheets out of my mind.* But she replied:

"I will, but if the questions will be quick I'd rather get it over with tonight. Otherwise I'll just be wondering about it for the next 12 hours…"

Joel: Again, I'm sorry to trouble you, but, yes, they're quick questions."

Wow. Even with text messaging, he uses excruciatingly correct punctuation, Maribelle thought. *He's pretty uptight, but I guess all accountants are.*

Maribelle: All right. Is it easier by phone call or text?

Joel: I'd rather call you, if that's OK.

Maribelle: Sure go ahead

The phone rang within seconds, but Maribelle let it ring three times before answering. She needed to say a quick prayer that she would answer Joel's questions correctly and with confidence. There wasn't anything to be nervous about because she hadn't done anything wrong. Or at least she hadn't done anything criminal; how she handled the books might point to a lack of competence or experience, but not fraud or any other criminal activity. She hoped Joel could see that.

"Hello, this is Maribelle."

"Hi, Ms. Reed. Again, so sorry to bother you."

"Please call me Maribelle. You don't have to be so formal."

"OK, thanks. Maribelle, as I said, I was looking over the spreadsheets and noticed some expenses that looked a little odd. I was hoping you could explain them."

"I'm not sure which ones would be 'odd,' but go ahead." She held her breath.

"The first one is a recurring item labeled BCJDF."

"Oh. Yeah." He *would* start with that one. Maribelle hesitated. She considered whether to explain the situation or have her employers do it. She decided on the latter. "I think you'd better ask Clem about that. It's a personal matter for him and Ginnie, and I don't feel comfortable being the one to share it with you."

"OK, I'll do that. You realize, though, that using the store's income to pay for personal items opens up a can of worms that you probably want to keep closed."

"I understand, and I agree that most personal items should be kept off the business' budget. But you'll just need to ask Clem about it tomorrow."

"I think I'll call him tonight after I go over the notes I'm taking now. I know that he and Ginnie haven't been getting to the store early since you took over as manager, and I don't see any need to ask them to arrive two frigid mornings in a row at the crack of dawn. We can speak privately tonight and go from there. Unless Clem wants to see the spreadsheets while we talk, I can just ask him to explain."

As he and Maribelle continued through Joel's list of questions, it became painfully obvious that she needed to educate herself further on bookkeeping for a business. It was one thing to learn how to create and maintain basic spreadsheets, but the information included in the spreadsheets could make or break a small business. She definitely had some learning to do. She hoped her ignorance didn't cause permanent harm to the store.

As they continued their analysis of the ledger, Maribelle's answers satisfied Joel … to a point. But he admonished her again that most of the line items he had brought up were better left off a business budget. Many of the expenses needed to be paid from Clem and Ginnie's personal checkbook, and perhaps they would need to sit down as a group and discuss best practices.

"Have Clem and Ginnie actually hired you?" Maribelle asked Joel. "When I talked to Ginnie this morning, she said it was kind of preliminary — that you were just taking a quick look at the books as a favor to them."

"I talked to Ginnie this evening, and we agreed that I need to take this on as a full-time project. So far what I've seen doesn't appear to be related to any fraud or have anything to do with the container full of unpaid invoices, but that still doesn't explain that tin of papers or why several of your vendors haven't been paid in months. Maybe tomorrow you could show me the accounts you pay online and the ones you pay by paper so that perhaps we can start to piece together this puzzle."

"No problem," Maribelle said. "Do you have any other questions?"

"Not tonight, no."

"Then I'm going to go reheat my cup of tea and get back to my book and my cat."

"Thanks for taking the time to talk to me tonight. Enjoy your tea and your cat."

After they hung up, Maribelle looked at her text messages again and was happy to see a reply about the cat brush.

Laney: Gosh I forgot to tell you! I was in a rush the other day after brushing Dickens and I absentmindedly took the brush with me. :(I saw it on my sofa table this afternoon as I was rushing out (again) for work and then class. Did I ever give you a key to my apartment?

Maribelle: No key and I'll probably be in bed when you get home tonight. Just bring it tomorrow please

Laney: I'm so sorry. ☹

Maribelle: No problem I'm sure we can find something that will do

The notion of using one of her own hair tools on her cat was a bit above and beyond the call of duty for this fur-mama, but she couldn't stand the kitty cold-shoulder any longer. Besides, she had been neglecting Dickens for months — since she became store manager, really — and it wasn't fair to deny him one of his favorite simple pleasures. What was a little cat hair between friends?

"C'mon, Dickens! Ready for a brush?"

She didn't have to ask him twice.

12

The rest of the Bedford Books staff could tell that something was not quite right. This was the Christmas season, and their employers weren't smiling.

That was unusual. Well, it was unusual for the Hatches. Maribelle was another story.

They sensed a tension in the air that made everyone walk on eggshells. Bethany was the first to say something.

"Maribelle, I know that Christmas isn't your favorite time of the year," the young woman said, "but this year you seem to be more tense than usual. Has being the manager been that stressful for you? Even Clem and Ginnie seem to have more on their minds this year."

Maribelle was glad that Bethany mentioned her being named store manager. She could focus on that instead of having to make excuses about the financial situation.

"You know, Bethany, I had no idea becoming Bedford Books' manager would cause me this much stress. I thought the bump in my paycheck would be nice, but there were things I didn't expect that have taken a huge toll on me."

Maribelle probably shouldn't have been confiding in another employee about the stressors of her job, but she had always been able to talk to Bethany and be assured she would keep their conversations just between them.

"Like what?" Bethany asked.

"Oh, you know, being responsible for so many things. Decisions that I sometimes made before, but only when Ginnie wasn't available to make them. Now they all seem to fall on my shoulders. She and Clem really have stepped back from a lot of things they used to handle alone."

"Is there anything I can do to help? I know that hearing from Jubilee that our printing bills were past due sure wasn't welcome news, on top of all your other regular responsibilities *and* the Christmas season, which I know you don't care for — or at least you *pretend* not to like," Bethany said, elbowing Maribelle in the arm.

Maribelle gave her friend a wry grin.

"Just having you as a friend and a reliable store employee helps more than you know, Bethany. I hope you know how much I appreciate you — and how much Ginnie and Clem appreciate you, too."

"That means a lot," Bethany said with a smile. "But if you need help with anything extra, you know where to find me."

"Thanks, B.B. We'll have to get together over a cup of tea after the holiday rush so you can tell me what you've been reading lately. I've been too busy to notice."

"Deal. I need to find out about your books, too."

"Ohhh, I can't wait to tell you about the one I just finished. You'd love it."

"Can't wait to hear about it."

It was nice to talk about books again — the kind you read for pleasure, not the ones you calculate in spreadsheets. Her session with Joel this morning had been brief because of the conversation they'd had last night. It was good they got that done before she arrived at 7 this morning, because the things he had discussed with the Hatches would take longer to show him once they opened the records again.

Maribelle had tried to call Clem and Ginnie last night with a heads-up as soon as she hung up with Joel, but apparently he beat her to it. She'd had to leave a message on their answering machine.

She hadn't wanted them to have to deal with these old painful memories as they got ready for bed last night — especially with Clem not feeling well — but it was probably better to get that over with, too. But before trying to reach them, she'd had another one of those internal battles she experienced frequently. Would they feel ambushed when Joel asked about BCJDF? (BCJDF was the juvenile defense fund for their nephew Billy that no one but the Hatches and Billy's parents knew about; he had made a youthful mistake, and they were making sure he got help.) Should Maribelle have tried harder to give Clem and Ginnie an opportunity to prepare before Joel confronted them?

But perhaps the words *ambush* and *confront* were too harsh to describe the conversation she knew they were going to have. Joel really did seem kind, even as he asked them all some tough questions that it was his job to ask. And she knew that he was in a situation no normal person would want to be in. He had been a complete gentlemen with the Hatches — and with her. She was glad they hadn't hired someone who turned out to be accusatory and who jumped to conclusions without solid evidence. Such people seemed to get pleasure from catching others in their misdeeds.

And, to this point, there was no hard proof of misdeeds; it was all circumstantial. But she sure would be glad when they found out why those unpaid invoices had ended up in that green and white tin hidden in the back of the desk.

She was grateful that Joel was a reasonable man and had not accused anyone — yet. Sooner or later he would, though. She just hoped it wasn't her. She hoped her shaky accounting skills didn't point the finger directly at her. With her strawberry blond hair, she was pretty sure she wouldn't look her best in prison orange. And she bet they wouldn't have a ready supply of peppermint tea for her, available whenever she requested it.

Maribelle really had let her imagination run wild the past few days. Speaking of peppermint tea, there didn't seem to be enough of it in the world to calm her nerves over the situation they were in.

She needed to read a good, relaxing book — a nice, clean romance with a happy ending instead of the mystery she had just finished.

She decided to ask Bethany for a recommendation. Maybe one of the books she'd been reading would be perfect for Maribelle this evening.

✳ ✳ ✳

"Has anyone seen Bethany?" Maribelle asked Ginnie and Todd, the college student who worked part time for Bedford Books.

"I saw her go into the office a few minutes ago," Todd said.

Maribelle thanked him and headed to the back.

"Hey, Beebs, whatcha doin'?" Maribelle asked her employee, who turned around suddenly from the desk.

"Oh, hi, Maribelle," B.B. said. "Oh, you know, not much. Just looking for wrapping paper."

Did she just hide something behind her back? Maribelle wondered, then immediately felt guilty. *Man, I need to get a grip. I'm becoming paranoid about everything!*

"OK. Well, I need a recommendation, and I know you can help me out. What's a great book you've read recently that will help me relax?

Nothing suspense or thriller — I need something calming and sweet. Something stress-relieving, ya know? I just finished a cozy mystery last night, and even it was a bit too much for me, even though most of those books are pretty tame."

"I hear ya, Mare. Let me think about it. A couple of books come to mind, but I'll thumb back through them and make sure there's nothing in either that would keep you up at night! You know I've been on a horror kick lately, right?"

"Yeah, that's why the caveat. Don't gimme no Stephen King or Dean Koontz. Or don't tell me you've found a holiday horror story — Killer Clowns Under the Christmas Tree?"

"Ha! No, but that would be totally awesome!" Bethany said with a gleeful look in her eyes.

She chuckled, mumbled something unintelligible and turned to leave the office, shoving something into her pocket as she went.

"I'll give you a reading list before quitting time. You got plenty of peppermint tea to go with it?"

"You know it! I look forward to your list. Thanks, Bethany."

Despite feeling guilty for being suspicious of Bethany's behavior, Maribelle took three steps into the room and stood at the desk, her eyes scanning every inch of the workspace. After all, since when did they keep wrapping paper in the office? Did Bethany really expect her to believe that's what she had been doing — looking for holiday gift wrap?

Maribelle was trying not to let this bookkeeping mystery ruin the Christmas season for her or the rest of the staff, but the mystery seemed to be winning, at the moment.

She really needed that good book and a nice, hot cup of peppermint tea. She and Dickens were overdue for a quiet, uneventful evening in front of their little 2-foot Christmas tree, watching snow gently fall outside their little window and listening to some Bing Crosby with the volume turned just high enough to set the mood.

It struck her that if she didn't rein in her imagination soon, the stress of the bookstore's financial situation, coupled with the everyday responsibilities that had been weighing her down all year, could become so prominent that she'd be in a bigger mess emotionally than she already was. Yep, she needed to rein it in fast, before it hit a full gallop and carried her down a path she didn't need to be heading down.

She whispered a quick prayer and committed to getting up 15 minutes earlier every morning to spend some time with the Lord so He could help her launch the day on the right trajectory.

And just as gently as the Lord had whispered to her a few days earlier, when her sour mood threatened to take over, another thought came to her mind:

Pick up your favorite book, Maribelle. It always helps you put things into perspective.

Why hadn't she thought of it before?

Besides the Bible, her favorite book was *The Hiding Place*, and it never failed to remind her of how blessed she was to live in a country where she was free to worship Jesus openly and without fear.

Not so for Corrie ten Boom and her Dutch family, or — in the same sense — for the Jews they hid inside a wall in their small house in Holland as Hitler's Nazi regime swept through Europe.

Maribelle had often taken her freedom of religion, and so many other things, for granted. The story of the ten Boom family and those they tried to save from the Nazis always brought her back to gratefulness for her own circumstances. Gratefulness … and often a sense of shame for being so cavalier about her blessings.

No more. Along with that commitment to God-time each morning, she committed to writing out her blessings, one by one. She would tape the handwritten list to her bathroom mirror so she could meditate on it each day — morning and night. Immediately she thought of things she could start putting on the list.

She was grateful for Christmas, despite appearances to the contrary. The season had always been special … until the one when she got her heart broken and she'd begun to succumb to bitterness. And the Christmas season could be special again this year. After all, it wasn't about trees and lights and wrapped packages and ceramic Santas. It was about the gift of Jesus, whose love and sacrifice brought healing and salvation to a needy and hurting world. Christmas was all the more special because of the people who had touched her life, and whose lives she touched. It was about making a difference in the world, together with those she served alongside every day.

Lord, Maribelle prayed. *Please help me be a light for your good news, not a source of stress or grief. Help me remind people of the real meaning of Christmas. You know how easy it is to become hurt and angry rather than positive and loving. Please help me conquer those negative emotions; I know they're not from You.*

I love You, Father, and I thank you for the gift of Jesus. Amen.

Maribelle breathed deeply and went looking for her coat. A nice walk in the sunshine was in order.

* * *

The little section of town where Bedford Books had landed nearly a century ago was one of Maribelle's favorite places.

When she was feeling social, she didn't mind getting out of her nearby apartment and away from her books and her kitty to amble down Bailey Street. She loved to look in the shop windows, say hello to friendly faces and enjoy the sights and sounds of the revitalized area that had become more of a tiny community than just a collection of streets and shops. It was no longer the rundown, forgotten area that the locals used to call Has-Bean Town.

At some point, the shop owners and other merchants had opened their eyes to the condition of the once-thriving four-block section of town and realized that it had been dying a slow death for years, right before their eyes. Collectively, they had begun to realize that this was not a case of bad business habits of the individual merchants, themselves.

This realization happened at a small gathering of shopkeepers around a 24-hour-diner table one morning — outside the area where their stores were located. Two of them had decided to meet for coffee one Saturday before their shops opened, another ran into them and sat down to chat "for just a minute," and, as happens most of the time when merchants get together, the talk quickly turned to "How's business?"

Before long, they realized that they weren't alone. The whole of Bailey Street was hurting and in danger of financial collapse if they let it continue the way it had been going.

They couldn't bear to see that happen, so they got together and formed a coalition — a mini-council — to see if they could save the area and their businesses.

With grants, guts and grunt work, the community pulled together a plan and started implementing it.

They called the initiative A Better Bedford.

Nowadays, Maribelle went to Bailey Street — even on her days off — to feel inspired and reinvigorated whenever she felt lonely. She didn't even fear walking along the streets after dark, because now most of the stores stayed open later and she knew most of the owners. Business had picked up, so closing at noon or 2 p.m. was no longer a necessity — it was an option. At this point, though, most of the owners still didn't exercise that option, maybe because the memory of the slow, lean days was still fresh.

There was new blood, too. Storefronts that once sat empty now boasted new owners, new facades and new offerings.

The store that once housed only a cake-decorating business had expanded to include scones, bagels, breakfast wraps and a coffee bar, enticing an early-morning crowd that had never stepped foot inside the business previously.

Success story after success story popped up around the area, and the merchants felt they had dodged a bullet by banding together to upgrade and reinvigorate Has-Bean Town.

But with progress comes problems, and A Better Bedford was experiencing its own growing pains.

The streets were getting less bicycle-friendly, and parking was becoming a bit of a challenge. Merchants who hadn't darkened the city council chambers before — whether because of complacence or denial — now had to show up and present their solutions to traffic, taxes and storefront standards.

Clem and Ginnie wanted to send Maribelle to these regular meetings, but she came back from the first one frustrated and refusing to go back.

Too much bickering, she said, and she didn't have time for small-minded, small-town politics. She respectfully declined to attend the next council meeting, asking the store's owners to relieve her of that duty forever.

She had felt guilty about that for a while, but she kept reminding herself that the Hatches were the owners — the ones who reaped the bulk of the store's profits — and their growing expectations of her responsibilities were starting to become unreasonable.

On her previous walk through the revitalized area of town, Maribelle had determined to talk to the Hatches about her work responsibilities.

Either cut me in on the profits directly (not just an annual salary bump that never amounts to much), or handle some of these responsibilities without me, she thought to herself.

Yes, she would do just that, she had decided.

She would talk to them.

As soon as the holidays were over, she was going to start on her novel in earnest, let Clem and Ginnie decide what duties they were willing to take over again (or hire another helper for Maribelle) and take back her life.

But all that was before this bookkeeping mess had reared its miserable head. Before she found the green and white tin crammed with old invoices.

Right now, she told herself, she needed to stroll up and down the streets in the fresh air and clean snow and enjoy the results of A Better Bedford as she tried to forget those worries for half an hour or so. And maybe she'd get a box of pastries from one of the shops to take back to the gang at Bedford Books.

13

Joel couldn't shake the feeling that he was missing something obvious.

Maribelle's accounting looked … amateurish. But he didn't detect anything criminal in her crude use of the spreadsheets. Obviously she had tried to replicate her employer's paper methods when she transferred the system to the computer in January. Maribelle was intelligent — he could tell that from previous conversations, even if she did seem a bit nervous and chattery every time they spoke — she just needed a little more formal training in bookkeeping matters.

But why did she always seem nervous when they talked? Was that her natural demeanor, or had the situation simply made her worry that he'd find something to accuse her of, even though so far she seemed to be guilty of nothing more than unconventional bookkeeping? Was she actually guilty of something?

But if she was guilty of something, what *was* that something?

Joel still needed to figure out exactly what was going on. Why were so many bills unpaid? Why was there a metal tin full of old invoices? How could the business still be operating under such circumstances?

None of it made any sense.

He called Clem.

"Who prepares your tax returns, Mr. Hatch?"

"We do it ourselves, son."

Well, that explained why Clem had called Joel to audit the store's books instead of calling his own accountant — Clem *was* his own accountant. Joel had been planning to ask the business owner why he wanted to hire him instead of summoning his usual CPA, but he had wanted to make a cursory examination of the books first; after all, he had seen plenty of outside firms take advantage of those who had hired them, and some had even paid legal consequences.

By the same token, he had seen his share of in-house financial misdeeds — employees stealing from those who had trusted them to keep a watch on their money.

Was that the case here? Joel was determined to figure that out. The Hatches were good people and, even though they trusted their new bookstore manager and his instincts told him that was justified, Joel had learned to trust no one and assume nothing — at least until he had evidence that they were trustworthy. That was kind of backwards of how he typically liked to live in his personal life, but it was a hazard of the job. He'd had to teach himself not to be gullible, but this had also forced him to guard against growing cynical in his work — and his relationships. The situation of the past few years certainly hadn't helped.

Lord, give me discernment, Joel prayed quickly before continuing his line of questioning.

"Do you pay quarterly estimated taxes?" Joel asked Clem.

"Yessiree. We always pay the government on time. We don't wanna get on the wrong side of Uncle Sam!"

"That's very wise, sir. Could I see your tax filings?"

"Sure, Joel. They're in the bottom-left drawer of my desk. I'll make sure they're ready for you to pick up. Will you be in the store today?"

"I'll make a point to drop by before lunchtime," Joel said. "Will you be there?"

"I don't know, son. I haven't been feeling well lately. I may stay home today."

"Sorry to hear that, sir. I hope you feel better soon. I'll get Maribelle to help me if I need something."

"That's fine, son. Good luck."

Clem sounded worn out. Joel bet the stress of this financial mystery was taking a toll on the aging businessman and his wife. After hanging up, he said a prayer for Clem's health, then poured himself a second cup of coffee and bent back over the tin of papers in front of him.

After a few seconds of incomprehension, he leaned back and stretched his legs in front of him as he ran his fingers through his thick, dark hair and rubbed his jaw. He couldn't seem to concentrate.

Maybe this is taking a toll on me, too. Am I getting too old for this? Am I letting my fondness for the Bedford Books staff — and particularly its manager — cloud my judgment?

Joel sighed and got up to look out the window.

Snow had begun to fall gently, quietly, beautifully, and he closed his eyes and imagined his mother. This was her favorite time of year, and she loved the snow.

✳ ✳ ✳

Maribelle couldn't seem to fix her mind on the tasks she needed to be doing this morning.

The gentle snowfall was distracting her.

In another life, Maribelle would have resisted the urge to pause and look out the window, but since coming to work for the Hatches, she had begun learning to "stop and smell the roses," sometimes literally. She took the time to do that now.

It had been a long time since Maribelle had allowed herself to notice and appreciate the beautiful, simple pleasures of life.

A bouquet of flowers, a sparkly snow globe, the sound of children's laughter, a gentle snow.

But lately, because she knew she would have to find small, daily ways to relieve stress or go crazy, she had forced herself to take in all the beautiful sights, sounds and smells of the Christmas season. Besides, she was getting older and she knew she would regret letting many more years go by as a harried, hurried worker bee. She had a great job working for great employers, a wonderful staff (most of the time) and too many blessings to count, and she had been taking it all for granted. She had finally begun to recognize that.

A few days earlier, she had started working on counting those blessings each morning, and it helped her start the day with gratitude instead of grumbling.

The snow was beautiful and serene.

Sometimes she thought she could smell the snowflakes from inside the store, just by watching them fall. She knew it was simply that the soft precipitation cleared the air — and her mind. The snow brought purity to the air and an accompanying, blessed sense of purity to her state of mind.

She wondered whether Joel was enjoying the snowfall on his side of town this morning.

The thought caused her to suck in a breath.

Why had she suddenly thought of Joel Stewart, and in such a sentimental way?

Wasn't he the enemy?

Well, that was stupid. Of course he wasn't the enemy; he was merely a fellow member of the local business community hired by her employers to help sort out a problem. But he sure made her nervous.

Was that because of the accounting mess at the store, though, or was it because he was so annoyingly handsome?

And tall.

And he smelled so good all the time.

And those green eyes …

Uh-oh.

This line of thinking would get her exactly nowhere that she needed to be going.

As Maribelle walked into the office to fetch a tea bag, the ringing phone startled her.

Who could be calling this early? It's only 7:15.

"Bedford Books, Maribelle speaking."

"Hello, Ms. Reed. It's Joel Stewart."

"Ummmmm, hello, Mr. Stewart."

"Please call me Joel, Ms. Reed."

"And you can call me Maribelle. Remember?"

As soon as the words were out of her mouth, she had second thoughts. It might be a bad idea for the two of them to start thinking of each other as anything more than business associates working to get to the bottom of an unpleasant financial situation. She hadn't thought of that the other night when Joel called her at home.

Nope, she didn't need to let her guard down around Mr. Joel Stewart, certified public accountant.

Possessor of the sparkling green eyes …

Maribelle was going to need therapy when this was all over. Probably a lot of it. And she'd better load up on the peppermint tea bags, just to be safe.

"OK, thanks. Maribelle, I talked to Clem this morning, and he told me where he keeps the quarterly tax filings. He said he'd have you get them for me to look over. I forgot to mention that I'll need the bank statements, too."

"I'll get you the tax papers, but the bank statements are all online now. We don't print them unless there's a problem that requires some scratching out on paper. … And, well, obviously there's a problem, so I'll make printouts of those for you. When will you be in?"

"I was thinking around 11 a.m. I won't be able to get there before your staff arrives this morning, so I thought I'd come and browse for a Christmas present and you could give me the printouts surreptitiously. If the packet is too big to hand to me without arousing suspicion, we could make up some excuse for me to visit the office for a moment and I'll put them in my briefcase."

"Maybe I could wrap them as a gift and have it ready when you get here, as though you had called ahead and ordered it. We sell children's backpacks, so maybe the size of the tax documents and the banks statements wrapped in a box would be of equivalent size to a small backpack. Do you have children?"

"A wrapped package is a brilliant idea, Maribelle," the accountant said. "And, no, I don't have children. I've never been married."

Joel wondered why he had felt the need to tack on that last sentence, but it was out before he could stop it.

"Neither have I," Maribelle said. She wasn't sure why she had asked about children or why she had told him she had never married.

This was getting way too personal.

"Maribelle?"

"Yes, Joel."

"I'll need to go over these documents on my lunch break because I have other commitments the rest of the day. Would you be available to join me for an hour, perhaps at a restaurant in the neighborhood? I'm likely to have questions."

"Questions? About me?" she stammered.

"Well, about your knowledge of the tax filings and the bank statements, yes."

"Oh. Yes. Yes, of course."

Maribelle was glad he couldn't see how red her face had just turned. Of course he was talking about the bookkeeping situation. Why had she suddenly thought (or secretly wished?) he intended to talk about personal things?

That was ridiculous.

"Ummmm, OK," she said after pondering the question. "As long as the store isn't too crowded when you get here. It is just a couple of weeks until Christmas, you know."

"I understand," Joel said. "We'll play it by ear. If you're not able to leave the store, we can talk about getting together later."

Why did the thought of "getting together later" with Joel make her blush? She was a grown woman, not a middle-school girl.

She was going to need a LARGE cup of tea.

14

When Joel arrived at the store just after 11 a.m., Maribelle already had Joel's "Christmas gift" secured in a box covered with purple and silver wrapping paper.

The gift-wrap was beautiful, secured with a shiny silver ribbon and topped with a large silver bow, and Maribelle wasn't sure why she had gone to all the trouble to make it look so special. For most gifts at Bedford Books, the staff took care to wrap them nicely, usually in shades of red and green, but this one was over-the-top beautiful.

Why? Maribelle asked herself. After all, it wasn't really a gift, and Joel was just going to rip into the fake package the minute he got out of the store.

Why the purple foil paper and silver ribbon? And why had she spent so much time and attention on it? It was silly.

But the minute the handsome, well-dressed accountant walked in, the realization hit her.

The handful of times she had been in Joel's presence, she couldn't remember seeing him in any color besides purple. She assumed it was his favorite color, but grown men usually didn't obsess about clothing details the way Joel seemed to.

His purple shirt, tie or sweater always looked good with the complementary colors he wore them with — navy dress slacks the first day, crisply pressed chinos the next, even a pair of dark-wash bluejeans with his cashmere turtleneck the last time.

But why always purple?

It must have been subliminal that she had chosen that color for Joel's faux gift. Apparently she associated him with purple.

Hmm. Oh, well. Whatever.

The more immediate puzzle, however, had her slightly paranoid:

Should she act like she knew Joel when he approached the sales counter? Should she wait for him to announce that he had "called in an order" for a Christmas gift? After all, they still hadn't told the rest of the staff that the CPA had been hired to audit the store's books. How would she explain knowing him? Any time the store was open during the holiday season, Bethany was there, so if Joel had visited previously as a customer, she would have known it — and remembered. That girl had the memory of an elephant.

Maribelle decided on Option 2 — Mr. Stewart had ordered the gift over the phone — and she'd follow his lead after that. She texted him the plan, but he hadn't responded before walking in. She was a terrible actress, but maybe she could pull it off.

"Good morning!" she sang cheerfully. "You must be the gentleman who called this morning. I'm Maribelle, the one who took your call."

"Yes, I'm Joel," the accountant replied.

"I have your gift wrapped and ready for you. I'll be right back with your purchase," she said before disappearing to the back.

Well, that went OK, Maribelle thought. *I didn't let my nerves cause me to babble and give everything away.*

But when she placed the purple and silver package into Joel's hands, she wasn't ready for his reaction — or her own.

His eyes widened, and he jerked his hand away when his fingertips brushed against the back of Maribelle's.

Joel appeared speechless. He stared at the package for a moment, then quickly recovered.

"Well, this will be perfect, Ms. Reed. My sister is sure to love it. Thank you for wrapping it so beautifully."

Maribelle was busy recovering from her own reaction to the slight touch of their fingers, but she sensed that there was more to Joel's actions than a mere jolt of romantic attraction. She couldn't put her finger on it, though.

"Hey, Mare, when did we get that purple wrapping paper? I've never seen it before. Have you been saving it for a special occasion?"

Maribelle's eyes shot daggers at Bethany, whose eyebrows shot up before she realized why her boss was so embarrassed. This tall, dark-haired man was gorgeous, and he looked like someone Maribelle could fall for with very little effort.

"Hello, sir. I'm Bethany." The young store clerk wasted no time in changing the subject. She reached over the counter and extended her hand to Joel.

"I hope the recipient of your gift enjoys whatever's in that package,"

Bethany said. "If not, you can return it any time before the end of January. We normally have a 30-day exchange policy, but for Christmas we add a week onto that because we know people are busy during the holidays. It's just a little extra-special touch we offer our customers. And if you ever need a good book recommendation — especially horror and suspense — I'm your girl. Just ask for me next time you come in. Bethany Bookworm, they call me around here."

Now who's babbling? Maribelle thought. *Well, at least she took the focus off that awkward moment.* Maribelle had to be grateful for that. And Bethany hadn't even known that the beautiful purple and silver package wasn't what it seemed.

"Would you like a bag for that, sir?" Maribelle asked Joel. "I could put your receipt in the bag for you."

"That would be great, Ms. Reed."

"I think I left the receipt in the office," she said. "I'll be right back." She cut Joel a look, and he nodded.

Once in the office, Maribelle quickly scribbled on a receipt pad, tore the page out and folded it so that no one but Joel could see what she had written:

"Meet you in 10 minutes at Difalso's? It's just north on Bailey Street. Best linguine in town."

Maribelle went back out and handed him a note, accompanied by a raise of her eyebrows and a slight nod that signaled, "Read it."

Joel read it, bid the two young women a merry Christmas, and walked out into the snowy day.

✳ ✳ ✳

"OK, Number 1," Maribelle said before she even took her coat off at the restaurant table where Joel was sitting. "We have to figure out a different way to do that next time — if there has to be a next time.

"That was just ... nauseating. I hate lying to the staff. I hate lying to anyone, but especially to people who trust me, and whom I trust. I'm a terrible actress, and I could feel Bethany trying to size up the situation the whole time we were putting on that little act. She's tack-sharp, and I doubt that she bought a word of it."

"And Number 2," she said, finally laying her red coat across her seat in the tapestry bench of their booth and planting herself across the white tablecloth from Joel. "I picked Difalso's because no one from Bedford Books ever comes here, except on special occasions. But after that fiasco, who knows? Bethany may just decide, after seeing that fancy purple wrapping paper, that today's snowfall is cause for a special celebration. The whole time we're sitting here, I'm going to be paranoid that she's about to walk in on us.

"And I won't be able to eat a thing. But thank you for requesting a table near the back."

"You're welcome. But I think you need to take a breath and relax, Maribelle," Joel said calmly. "So far I haven't found anything conclusive in your store's records. And, even if I do, it won't be long before I start interviewing the entire staff — at least until I find some solid evidence that a particular person is responsible for the imbalance. And then everyone will know who I am."

"You haven't found anything conclusive? You've been poring over those records for days now. Why haven't you figured out what's going on?"

"For one thing, I haven't been given access to all the records," he said, a slight hint of accusation in his voice.

"The only thing that's left is what you have in that pretty purple package. Have you opened it yet?"

"Just about to," Joel replied.

The waiter approached and asked for their beverage orders while placing a basket of Italian bread between them. Maribelle nudged it closer to Joel, looking as though she wanted to eat the whole thing but thinking about how difficult it had already been to pull her Christmas tights over her thighs and hips that morning.

"Just water for me," Joel told the waiter.

"Do you happen to have any peppermint tea?" said his companion.

"No, signora, mi scuso."

Joel breathed a quiet sigh of relief.

"Oh. Well, just some iced tea, per favore." She tried to hide her disappointment, but she could really use a cup of her favorite tea.

"Very well, ma'am."

When the waiter was out of sight, Maribelle looked at Joel expectantly.

"Well?"

"Well, what?" Joel hadn't known Maribelle long enough to read her mind, and, he told himself, he wasn't likely to acquire that skill, no matter how long they knew each other. For a brief moment, thoughts of a potential future with Maribelle flashed through the accountant's mind. He cleared his throat and pulled at his dark gray necktie.

"The package," Maribelle reminded him. "Not that I expect it to help you solve the mystery, but it's the only thing we have left."

"I agree that the tax documents aren't likely to answer all the questions, but I have one question for you: Have you called all the vendors about the past-due bills?"

"Well, no, we — " The question stopped Maribelle in midsentence. "Gee, I guess I thought we needed direction from you before we started calling them. Now I realize that was a stupid assumption. I should've talked to you about it. Do you think it would make a difference?"

"Yes, I do, for two reasons: First, it's the right thing to do. Even if they aren't willing to work with you on a payment plan, they still need to hear from you. Your employers need to apologize for allowing the situation to happen — however it happened — and let the vendors know you're willing to do whatever it takes to make it right. If you're a praying woman, you could start with that, in fact. Pray for the Lord to give you favor with your creditors."

"That makes so much sense," Maribelle said. "And, yes, I do pray. I seek the Lord's favor every day in my personal life and in my dealings with people. Thank you for helping me realize that we should do that with the business."

Joel smiled. Maribelle wasn't sure why, but she hoped it was because he'd discovered that she was a fellow believer. She certainly was grateful that she now knew that fact about him.

"You said you had two reasons we should call the creditors ..."

"You probably haven't thought about this, but maybe you'll discover that the situation isn't as dire as you assume," Joel continued.

"I've audited a lot of businesses, Maribelle, and something about this one just seems odd. It doesn't have the hallmarks of criminal activity or deception. I can't exactly put my finger on it, but there's something we're missing."

"I guess that should make me feel better, Joel, but I still don't think I'm going to get a good night's sleep until we figure it out."

"I understand, and I'm working as hard as I can to decipher the meager clues you've given me."

"I appreciate that, Joel." Maribelle reached out and touched his hand, and he let it linger for a second before withdrawing it and picking up his napkin.

After a moment of awkward silence, the waiter brought their drinks and took their food orders. He looked at Maribelle first.

"Veal parmigiana, per favore," she said.

"An excellent choice, signora," the waiter said, then turned to Joel without writing anything down.

"I hear you have the best linguine in town," Joel said.

"Si, signore, you can't go wrong with Difalso's fresh, homemade linguine."

"How about linguine with clam sauce, if that wouldn't be too prosaic."

"Another excellent choice. And some wine, signore?"

"No, thank you."

"Very good, sir." The waiter departed, and Joel and Maribelle were left to decipher their financial puzzle in private.

Maribelle had been to Difalso's a handful of times, always for special birthday or anniversary celebrations with her family — and when she got the promotion to bookstore manager.

Never with a date.

But Joel wasn't a date, she reminded herself. This was a professional meeting to discuss an unfortunate situation, and Joel didn't think of Maribelle as anything but a client — or, more precisely, the employee of a client. His presence in her life was strictly for business, and as soon as he helped Bedford Books' owners solve the mystery of the unpaid invoices, he and she would go their separate ways.

Joel looked around the room as if for the first time.

"This is a nice place, Maribelle. Thank you for suggesting it. I've been eating sandwiches at my desk far too often lately."

He could envision sitting in this booth with Maribelle under less-stressful circumstances someday. Of course, it would be more dimly illuminated with candlelight in the evenings, and with the restaurant's house lights turned way down, he could tell. Joel was glad the candles weren't flickering now, though. Besides the fact that he and Maribelle would have trouble seeing the bank documents in dimmer light, the presence of a romantic glow would be far too distracting. It would cast her beautiful pale blue eyes in a more intoxicating light, and he certainly didn't need that distraction.

They had work to do.

"Joel?"

"Yes?"

"I just realized something: You're not wearing purple today. Every time I've seen you before today, you have on some shade of purple. In fact, I think it must be why I wrapped your 'gift' in purple," Maribelle smiled sheepishly.

Joel stuck his leg out to the side of the booth and hitched up his pants leg.

Purple socks.

Maribelle's laugh lit up her eyes.

She was about to ask Joel to explain his purple obsession when the waiter brought an appetizer and refilled their water glasses. At that moment, she realized she was ravenous, and she couldn't wait to dig in. Spending a few minutes with Joel in this quiet and cozy setting had a pleasant effect on her nerves, and she thought she could eat the entire dish set before her.

15

Once Joel had the beautiful purple package unwrapped, carefully saving the bow, as his grandmother always did, he dug through the box looking for the files he had requested.

"Didn't I mention that I needed the bank statements, Maribelle?"

Maribelle gasped.

"Oh, no! I should have called to tell you, but I got interrupted by a customer phone call when I realized: "The bank statements are missing!"

"They're what?" Joel looked at her uncomprehendingly.

"I logged onto the computer to print them for you, and my Bedford Bank folder was gone from the accounting folder. I don't know what happened to it."

Joel narrowed his eyes.

"And this little piece of trivia just slipped your mind?" the accountant said, his patience starting to wear thin. First the hemming and hawing over the personal files, and now this.

"I know it makes me look guilty, despite what you said a few minutes ago about not suspecting anything criminal, but it's the truth. I don't know what else to say."

"Well, the fact that you withheld this information from me until now does give me cause for concern, Ms. Reed."

Ouch.

So they were back to courtesy titles and surnames.

"*Mr. Stewart*," Maribelle emphasized. "I understand that this looks a tad 'convenient' on my part, but I truly was trying to provide good service to my customers in this busy holiday season while trying to find information for your audit. Juggling it all has proved to be a challenge, to put it mildly. We can get some of the bank statements back, but only those from last month, plus the transactions that have occurred between the last statement and close of business yesterday. We bank at a small, family-owned institution, and Bedford Bank doesn't have the bandwidth to store all its customers' statements for all time.

"I already called the bank before you arrived at the store this morning, and the tech people informed me that they went through a transition of their archival system recently, and they had a few hiccups. They're going to see if they can help me reconstruct some of the information we're missing. But I assure you, there was no ill intent in failing to disclose this information to you before now."

"What about the fact that the bank statements went missing in the first place?" Joel said, his expression still skeptical.

"I don't know," Maribelle said quietly, her eyes down and her chest getting tight. "Again, I know it doesn't look good. But I guess that's another mystery you're going to have to look into."

"One of the things I haven't pushed you on, Maribelle" — *oh, good, they were back on a first-name basis* — "is your continued assertion that only you, Clem and Ginnie have access to the files. Do you keep all the physical files locked up and the electronic files password-protected when you're not in the office?"

"Well ... most of the time. We've always trusted each other — the entire staff — and no one has ever seen the need to treat the bookstore like Fort Knox."

"I don't mean to be harsh, Maribelle, but that's going to have to stop."

"Actually, it already has. I changed the passwords to the computer and to the folder where I keep the accounting spreadsheets. I also learned how to password-protect the individual spreadsheet files."

"What about the desk where the paper documents are kept?"

"That's next on the list. Clem lost the key to the desk several years ago, so we're going to start keeping the sensitive papers in the safe, where we keep the cash at night."

"Please tell me you keep the safe locked during the day, too, when other employees — and customers — are around?" Joel said, a with hopeful tone.

"We do now."

Maribelle looked as though she could burst into tears at any moment.

Joel leaned back and ran his slender fingers through his hair.

"When do you expect to hear back from the bank about the historical transactions?" he asked.

"They said someone would get back to me by the end of the week."

"*The end of the week?* That's not soon enough, Maribelle. We need those documents *now*. Is there anything we can do to hurry them along? I'd like to have that information today, if it's at all possible."

"You have to understand, Joel. A lot of banking business rises and falls with the retail seasons, just like bookstores and electronics stores and toy stores and a ton of other merchants trying to keep their businesses afloat. We don't take a break around the holidays, like accountants and landscapers can. This is our — and the banks' — busiest season. For some, it's their make-or-break season. We can't expect our bank to drop everything for us just because we have a crisis."

"That's a good point, Maribelle. I'm sorry." Joel's tone softened. "We'll just have to find a way to figure some of this out while we wait. In the meantime, did you bring *any* printouts from the bank?"

"It was on my to-do list, and, trust me, I wasn't treating it cavalierly. It's just that we had this persnickety customer who called and wanted a backpack for his kid sister, and he wanted it wrapped all fancy-like, in shiny paper, ya know. I had to drop everything and devote extra time to it so the customer wouldn't report me to the Christmas-gift police."

Joel laughed, and it reached his eyes.

Maribelle took a deep, relieved breath; she had made him laugh.

Maybe that next cup of peppermint tea could wait.

✳ ✳ ✳

Maribelle and Joel spent the next few minutes looking at documents that didn't help them get any closer to answering their bookkeeping questions.

At about the time they reached the conclusion that they were only going to continue to frustrate themselves if they didn't take a break, their mouth-watering entrees arrived, along with a fresh basket of Italian bread accompanied by a dish of olive oil and roasted garlic for dipping.

Joel took a bite of his linguine and sat back in his chair, eyes closed.

"You weren't kidding about the linguine," he sighed.

"I would never lie about carbohydrates and garlic," Maribelle said, grinning as she confessed two of her favorite food groups. "But I'd better not mention the tiramisu. You might die of happiness, and we need to keep you alive until we get out of the woods with our creditors."

Joel chuckled, but his eyes were wide open.

"Maribelle, I know how upsetting this is to all of you. It's upsetting to me, too. I hate to see good people go through the stress you all have been under lately. But I want you to know that I'm doing my best to try to help you figure it out and fix it. It's got me flummoxed, and I don't like being flummoxed."

"I appreciate that, Joel. It has been stressful, and I know you're trying to help. Clem and Ginnie know how hard you're working to help them … us." Maribelle looked into Joel's eyes, and at that moment she felt she could trust him with anything.

In fact, looking into his eyes made her want to bare her soul to this man. She realized, at that exact moment, that she was starting to see him as more than an accountant — even as more than just an incredibly handsome man who wore intoxicating aftershave and had the deepest green eyes she had ever seen.

That thing about dressing in purple every day? That was intriguing, and she planned to ask him about it when this was all over.

Not now, though. Right now, there was work to do, and she was determined to get this mystery solved soon so they could all enjoy Christmas as the Savior's birth was meant to be celebrated — with loved ones, reminding the world of the extravagant Gift they had been given by God.

✳ ✳ ✳

When Maribelle arrived back at the store from lunch, she looked for her employer.

"Ginnie, did the bank call while I was out?"

"No, dear. What were they supposed to call about?"

"Well, I'm not sure we should expect them to call today; I was just hoping," Maribelle said. "We were so busy before Joel and I went to lunch, I didn't have time to tell you: I couldn't find this year's bank statements on the computer. We get them electronically and I never print them, so it's really unfortunate — and a mystery — that they're gone. Joel needs them because he's not coming up with any answers based on what we've given him so far. The bank keeps a limited archive of customers' statements, and their IT department is working to see if they can find some that go farther back than last month."

"Oh, dear," Ginnie sighed. "I wonder what could have happened to the bank statements. Do you have any idea?"

"That's the big mystery, Ginnie. Someone would have had to go in and deliberately delete them. The person would have to know how to work a computer, and you, me and Clem are the only ones with access. I realize that this whole mess casts me in a bad light, because I'm the one responsible for the store's finances."

"You are not totally responsible for our finances, my dear," the kind woman said. "Clem and I have ultimate responsibility, and we may have given you more to bite off than you could chew this year. We are the ones responsible for that."

"Ginnie, I was going to talk to you and Clem after the holidays about my workload, but I didn't want it to be because I had let you down. I feel so terrible about this whole situation. I'm just sick about it."

"Nonsense. Clem and I love you, and we trust you, Maribelle. Don't you forget that."

"But how could you, Ginnie? People cheat their employers all the time. How do you know I'm not the one who hid the tin of papers and then suddenly 'discovered' them — for whatever weird reason?"

"I think you'd need to be a better actress than you are, my darling. No offense, but you're not known for being able to keep things to yourself. I don't mean you aren't trustworthy with confidential information; I just mean that you aren't as good at hiding your feelings as you think you are — at least to me." Ginnie smiled.

Maribelle took a moment to process that. She thought she had become a master at keeping her emotions in check. At least that had always been her aim — since her broken engagement, anyway. After her fiancé broke off their engagement two years ago, she had realized that some people couldn't handle honesty, even from the people they supposedly loved. Maribelle was careful about whom she let see her vulnerabilities. She hoped that Ginnie was one of the few people who saw through her. She wondered about Clem, but even if he didn't pick up on things firsthand, no doubt Ginnie had confided in him about certain things. After all, they needed to have a good handle on their Number 1 employee; she ran their store.

Maribelle couldn't say that keeping her emotions close to the vest had actually served her well these past couple of years. It had simply become a habit she couldn't seem to break, even though she knew she could trust people like Ginnie, Clem and Bethany.

Besides her parents, the three of them knew her the best and were always supportive and patient with her, even when she didn't deserve it. And for the past 11 months, her not-deservingness had gotten a bit out of hand.

Even Clem and Ginnie's trust in her seemed too much to expect. If the situation were reversed, would she assume the best of either of them? It pained her to even think it, but maybe, maybe not.

"It's funny, Ginnie. Joel seems to trust me, too. Unless he's a really good actor — better than I am, apparently! — he doesn't suspect me of doing anything wrong. I don't know why. I would be suspicious of everyone until I had proved them innocent."

Ginnie smiled again. "I think he just has good instincts, sweetheart. I'm sure he's using his instincts and his training to make sure he doesn't overlook anything. But if he hasn't given you any cause to worry, then I wouldn't worry."

"Easy for you to say. You're not the one who let the accounting records disappear. I still feel responsible, even if I didn't do anything criminal."

Before Ginnie could reply, the phone rang and she picked it up after the first ring.

"Why, hello, Joel. Maribelle and I were just talking about you. ... Yes, the audit is the only thing on all of our minds these days — at least the three of us. It's been difficult to keep this private; our little Bedford Books staff is like family, every one of us. ... Yes, I understand. We'll just be glad when you get to the bottom of the mystery and this is all over."

Joel asked about Clem.

"He's ... tired. That's the only word I can think of to describe it. He's not eating much, and I'm pretty concerned about him. The bookkeeping mess is serious, of course, but he seems to be letting the situation upset him disproportionately. We've always been able to take hardships in stride, trusting in the Lord to guide and strengthen us. But Clem's strength seems to be a rare commodity these days. ... Thank you, Joel. I'll give him your love. Here's Maribelle."

After polite greetings, Joel said to Maribelle, "Do you get Saturdays off?"

"I try to. If one of our regular staff calls in sick and no one else can fill in, I have to cover, but otherwise I have Saturdays for personal time. Why do you ask?"

"I know the store is incredibly busy this time of year, and you have the usual stressors on top of the accounting situation and Clem's fatigue that's preventing him from helping out at the store, but I also know that you'd all like to get to the bottom of this. The alternative to meeting outside of normal working hours is we drag things out until after your Christmas rush is over.

"I'd like to sit down with you and go over everything we have," he said. "I know we can't do it at the store, so perhaps we could find a place to meet — maybe the Bedford Library? I'd offer the conference room at my agency, but no one else is likely to be there on a weekend this close to Christmas. I don't think it would be appropriate for us to be there alone together."

"The library has study rooms with glass walls," Maribelle said. "Would that work? And what about tonight? No reason we should wait until Saturday if you're available this evening."

"That would be perfect, actually, especially if we could reserve a room with a large table or desk to spread everything out on."

"I'll call the library as soon as we hang up and see about reserving a room. Would you like Ginnie to be there, assuming she can?"

"I think it would be great if Ginnie could be there — and Clem, if he feels up to it. But I understand that you can't leave the store understaffed for too long, and that Clem's health is a consideration."

Maribelle put her hand over the phone and explained the conversation. Ginnie said to let Joel know she would be there, but she would have to check with Clem as to whether he'd try to make it.

"Joel, I'll let you know about the library. Ginnie and I will definitely meet you."

"Perfect," Joel said. "I look forward to hearing back when you find out about the study room."

16

Ginnie thought about waiting until she took a late lunch break to call Clem and check on him, but then she remembered: *It's two weeks 'til Christmas; I don't get a lunch break!*

She dialed their home number and waited for Clem to answer.

When the answering machine picked up, she left a message:

"Hello, sweetheart. I hope you're feeling better. Call me at the store when you get this. I need to discuss something with you. Love you, sweetie!"

It wasn't like Clem to ignore the phone when he was home. Perhaps she had caught him in the shower or he was in some other way indisposed. She'd give him a few minutes, hoping he'd notice the blinking light on the answering machine.

Meanwhile, one of Ginnie's favorite customers had entered the store while she was phoning Clem, and she walked out to greet the woman and her granddaughter.

"Ava, it's so good to see you! And I see you brought your grandmother," Ginnie said as she hugged her old friend and picked up 3-year-old Ava for a kiss and a hug. Ginnie always greeted the children first, even when she and the grown-ups were longtime friends.

"Ava, I have a new book you're going to love; it's all about ice skating!"

Ava's squeal could be heard from the heavens, no doubt. The child was obsessed with ice skating. She wriggled out of Ginnie's arms and headed for the children's section. "Show me! Show me!" she ordered Ginnie as she ran toward her favorite stacks. "Hurry!" she demanded in her sweet little voice as she looked back at the two women, who obviously were not aware of the urgency.

"We'd better hustle, Judith. I don't think she's going to let us chat until she's picked up that book."

Judith chuckled as she followed Ginnie to catch up with her excited granddaughter.

* * *

As the afternoon hustled on, December shoppers busily asking about new volumes and needing suggestions for "the perfect gift for ...," Ginnie didn't have a lot of time to worry about Clem's lack of a return phone call. Maybe he had called back and one of the store employees had answered but been too busy to let Ginnie know. They were all busy.

Good thing, too, because who knew what sort of shape the store's finances were really in? Joel needed to get them some answers soon, so that they could sort out whom and to what extent they might owe.

Ginnie was an optimist, but she had to admit to herself that the store's financial situation and Clem's recent fatigue had her concerned. She wondered whether Clem's physical state had more to do with his mental state — worrying about the store — or some physical condition they needed to get checked out. He was forgetting things, too, but that came with age. Age, and stress.

She would talk to him tonight, because she had heard too many stories of, "I'll go to the doctor after the holidays" or "I'll get checked out after I've met my deadline." Usually the stress of holidays, deadlines and such only made things worse, not better.

She would always regret not insisting that her brother see a doctor sooner, as an earlier diagnosis might have prevented some of the invasive and devastating cancer treatments he had experienced. His surgery was two years ago, but the physical and mental effects of it still lingered.

And then there was the reality that no one is promised tomorrow, and Ginnie wanted to be sure that everyone she came in contact with heard the good news of the gospel. Tomorrow might be too late.

Clem had a solid, longtime relationship with Jesus, so that wasn't a concern, but he was her husband and that was cause enough for her to be proactive about his condition — whatever that might be.

She promised herself that she would not put off the conversation; they would talk tonight, and she might even make him an appointment with their doctor tomorrow — holidays or no.

* * *

When Maribelle arrived at the Bedford Library, Joel was already in the small study carrel she had managed to procure, making one more pass over the papers already in his possession. Maribelle hadn't been able to get either of the large study rooms because this was finals week at the local university, and harried students had snatched up the two larger rooms to study in groups long before Maribelle inquired about them.

Ginnie had been unsuccessful in reaching Clem before Maribelle left to meet Joel, so the young manager left her employer at the store with Bethany, Todd and Adam, the temporary helper they had hired for the holiday season. Ginnie was worried about Clem and told Maribelle that she would just have to represent her employers at the meeting with Joel; Ginnie wanted to get home as soon as possible to check on her husband. They were all hoping that Joel and Maribelle could make progress on the situation, perhaps managing to solve it today — even before the bank came through with archived statements.

Joel's brow was furrowed when Maribelle walked in and closed the door, and he cut to the chase without so much as a greeting.

"Maribelle, I've been trying to remain objective and not reach any conclusions without seeing all the evidence, but I'm still at a loss," the accountant said. "I'm eager to see the bank transactions you've been able to pull together."

Maribelle pulled out what she had — meager though it was. Joel took the few pages and spread them out on the small desk to examine.

They spent the next few minutes examining the transactions, but they were no closer to enlightenment than they had been when Maribelle pulled the tin out of the desk drawer a few days earlier.

"Maribelle, let's call it a night," Joel finally said. "I know that you're worried about Clem and would like to call Ginnie to check on him. And I think we're just spinning our wheels. I know I could use a break. I need to start fresh on it in the morning, and perhaps the bank will have some answers for us."

Joel was right on all counts, and, as much as Maribelle wanted to figure out the bookkeeping mess and put it all behind them — no matter how it turned out — she needed to go home to Dickens, have dinner and take a nice, relaxing bubble bath before hitting the hay.

Things would look better in the morning, she tried to convince herself.

When Maribelle looked at her phone, she realized Ginnie had tried to reach her. She had called Maribelle half an hour earlier, but

Maribelle had turned her phone to silent mode when she arrived at the library. Apparently the vibration from the incoming call hadn't been intrusive enough to get Maribelle's attention.

She listened to the semi-frantic message from Ginnie.

"Maribelle, please call me as soon as you can. I've just arrived home, and Clem isn't here. The front door is unlocked, and he's nowhere to be found. I'm going out to look for him."

"Oh, no," Maribelle said to Joel. "I need to get to Ginnie's. She can't find Clem. She left a voice message for me 30 minutes ago."

"Why don't you call her back before you jump to conclusions?" Joel said. "She may have found him by now."

"Don't you think she would have let me know if she had?" Maribelle was trying to keep her voice calmer than her insides felt.

"Depends. Just call her."

Maribelle hit Ginnie's number on her speed dial.

Voicemail.

"I'm going," she told Joel.

"Let me drive you," he said.

When they reached Joel's car, he opened the door for Maribelle and waited until she climbed in, then he closed it before going around to the driver's side. Even through her worry, she took note of the thoughtfulness of that gesture. She wondered whether it was because she looked vulnerable tonight, or did he always open doors for ladies? She supposed this was the first time he had been in a position to open a door of any kind for her, and she decided that she could get used to this kind of treatment.

✳ ✳ ✳

When they arrived at the Hatches' house, they found Ginnie's car out front instead of in the garage. *Well, at least we didn't find any police cars here*, Maribelle said to herself. She had been trying not to imagine any worst-case scenarios on the excruciating drive from the library.

As they got out and walked up the sidewalk to the front door, Maribelle stopped and put her hand on Joel's arm.

"I'm afraid to ring the bell. Before we do, would you mind stopping to say a quick prayer with me?" she asked him.

"Of course, Maribelle. Would you like me to pray?"

"Yes, that would be so nice, Joel."

He took her hands in his, and she was immediately comforted by his warmth as they stood in the cold.

"Father, we praise you for knowing everything about us, including what is happening with Clem and Ginnie right now. We ask you to protect them and keep them safe. Calm Maribelle's nerves, no matter what we discover. Help us to support the Hatches in any way we can. We pray in your Son's name. Amen."

Maribelle could have cried, she was so grateful for Joel's quick and heartfelt prayer. She felt closer to him in that moment than she had in any of the preceding days. "Father, thank you," she breathed silently while her eyes remained closed. "He's a good man, and I'm grateful to have him here with me to face this situation, whatever it is."

"Ready?" Joel asked as he gave her hands a quick squeeze.

Comfort and joy.

"Ready."

He let go of Maribelle's hands and pressed the doorbell.

At first Maribelle thought no one was going to answer. She strained to hear any hint of a sound from inside.

Finally, Ginnie opened the door.

"Oh, Maribelle, I'm so glad you came!" Ginnie said. "Come inside."

Joel and Maribelle moved inside and stood in the warm entryway with Ginnie.

The bookstore owner's face was strained; she looked as if she could burst into tears at any moment.

"What happened, Ginnie? What's going on? Where's Clem?" Maribelle said, trying keep her words gentle and not demanding.

"He's sitting in his recliner in front of the fire, acting like nothing has happened. I found him in the backyard, sitting in one of the patio chairs, in the dark. He wasn't wearing a coat or shoes, Maribelle."

"What? What was he doing out there?" Maribelle said.

"He said he went out to feed the squirrels. I don't know what he thought he was feeding them, but I didn't see any signs of squirrels, or acorns, or any evidence that any animals had been on the patio since I swept it over the weekend. It was just Clem, coatless and shoeless, and I have no idea how long he was out there. He was half-frozen when I found him. He was shivering, but he didn't even seem to notice how cold he was."

"What in the world, Ginnie?" Maribelle said.

Joel hadn't said a word since they stepped inside. Maribelle couldn't read his expression, but his green eyes seemed sad, with a distant look.

"I don't know, Maribelle, but this confirms that I need to get him checked out. I was already planning to call the doctor and make an appointment for him. He just hasn't been acting himself lately. Now I wonder if I should take him to the emergency room tonight."

Joel finally spoke, but his voice was soft: "Is he acting like what you would consider normal now?"

"Yes, completely normal," Ginnie said. "When he finally stopped shivering, he asked if I wanted him to fix me some dinner because I looked tired. Then he gave me a hug, just as if nothing had happened."

Joel didn't say anything; he just continued to stand in the foyer looking pensive.

Finally he said, "Is this the first time anything like this has happened?"

"Well, nothing to cause this level of concern before tonight, but he has been acting very distracted lately. At first I thought it was the normal stress of the holiday season at the store. Then Maribelle found the mystery tin, and we added an extra layer of worry on top of the usual Christmas stress."

"Hmm," Joel said.

"What are you thinking, Joel?" Maribelle asked.

Before he could answer, Clem appeared in the doorway to the living room.

"Maribelle, Joel! Nice to see you tonight! Would you like some dinner? I was about to scrounge up something to fix for Ginnie. She's been under so much stress lately."

The trio looked at Clem, then one another. No one said a word.

"Why, you *all* look worried," Clem said. "Come in and sit down; I'll feed all four of us! I'm actually kind of hungry, myself."

He turned and headed toward the kitchen.

"See?" Ginnie said to the pair left standing with her, staring after Clem.

"Joel?" Maribelle said. She wanted to know what he knew — or thought he knew — about Clem's behavior.

"Ginnie," Joel said. "I think your husband is probably OK for tonight, but you probably will want to make an appointment first thing in the morning. Do you have my phone number? If you need anything tonight, I want you to call me, even if you think it's trivial."

"What makes you say this, Joel? You seem to have had experience with this kind of behavior," Ginnie said.

"My mother was ill for a few years, and it just seems familiar," he said.

"Ill with what?" Ginnie prompted, trying not to give her imagination free rein.

Joel hesitated, that sad look back in his eyes. "I think anything I say would be premature, Ginnie."

"It's too late for that, Joel. You've already demonstrated that you're concerned. I need to take care of my husband, and I need to know what you think might be wrong. What illness did your mother have?"

Joel closed his eyes for a moment, then opened them and looked at Ginnie, not wanting to say the words. But he must.

"She had Alzheimer's disease."

17

As soon as Ginnie woke up the next morning, she rolled over and reached for Clem.

He wasn't there.

She got up and cinched her pale blue bathrobe around her waist, scuffing into her slippers faster than she normally would. She headed for the thermostat; it was so cold in the house.

"Clem?" she called tentatively from the hallway.

"Yes, dear."

Relief washed over Ginnie when she heard her husband's familiar voice. She hadn't slept much last night, and when she did the slumber was fitful and full of troubled dreams in which Clem disappeared forever — sometimes willingly and at other times through circumstances not of his choosing.

She wondered what had caused him to "disappear" yesterday and what surprises the coming day would hold.

The sun hadn't appeared on the horizon yet, so she knew it would be a couple of hours before she could call the doctor's office to see if they'd be able to squeeze in a visit.

Ginnie found Clem in his recliner close to the fire, the same place he had sat last night after she collected him from outside.

"How are you, love?" she said to her husband of 45 years. Seeing him relaxed in his chair in front of the fireplace, as she had seen him dozens — no, hundreds — of times made tears well in her eyes. Everything looked normal, but she knew that everything was certainly *not* normal.

"Wonderful, sweetheart. The coffee's made, nice and strong, just like you like it."

Ginnie hadn't been able to get the word "Alzheimer's" out of her mind since last night. She hoped with all her heart that Joel was wrong. This morning, Clem remembered how she preferred her coffee, and he had put a pot on before she got up. That was completely normal.

But if it wasn't Alzheimer's, was it something worse? What could be worse?

A brain tumor?

She stopped herself. No use letting her imagination run wild. They just needed to see the doctor and let him perform a thorough examination of her husband.

"I'll grab a cup and join you in a minute. Be right back," Ginnie said to the love of her life.

Clem smiled at her — the smile that had stolen her heart when they were teenagers and still sent a thrill through her entire body — then he turned back toward the fire.

She paused a moment and watched him, then hurried to the kitchen before he could see the tears that rimmed her eyes and threatened to spill over onto her cheeks.

"Lord," Ginnie breathed as she leaned against the coolness of the ceramic tile countertop, the smell of coffee waking up her senses. "Lord God, we need you now. Forgive me for letting holiday busyness get in the way of my prayer time these past few days. You know that's a tendency of mine — to put other things before you. But please remind us of your presence with us. We so desperately need you.

"I don't know what's going on with the bills at the store, but at this moment that's not important to me. Something is obviously wrong with Clem, and I ask you for answers — soon. Don't let my imagination get the better of me. Give me a clear mind so that I can help him. Help us get an appointment this morning with the doctor, and guide the doctor and his staff to find answers.

"I love you, Lord," Ginnie whispered. "Thank you for how you're going to take care of us. In Jesus' name, amen."

With one hand, Ginnie wiped the tears that had been streaming down her cheeks as she prayed. With the other hand, she poured a cup of coffee, stuffed a tissue into the pocket of her fuzzy bathrobe and headed back to the living room to sit with Clem.

"It's such a cold, crisp morning," he said to his wife.

"Have you been outside again?" Ginnie tried to keep her voice calm.

"No, but I stood and looked out the bay window in the dining room. We're supposed to get a little snow today. It's beginning to look a lot like Christmas!"

The joy on Clem's face melted his beloved's heart. He was like a kid at … well, Christmastime. She knew that Clem's childlike enthusiasm was the reason he connected so well with their younger customers at Bedford Books. She thanked God for her husband.

✻ ✻ ✻

"Dr. March is booked solid today, Mrs. Hatch," the medical assistant said. "So many people have come down with the flu this month. We've had our hands full just taking care of them. That doesn't even account for routine visits and other patients we've needed to see."

"Isn't there some way you can get Clement in to see him? He really needs to be evaluated," Ginnie said, although she wasn't hopeful that it would be today.

"Tell you what: I'll put you on the waiting list. If you can be ready to bring him in at a moment's notice, we'll see what we can do."

"I'll take any crumb you can throw me! Thank you so much."

When Ginnie hung up the phone, she took a deep breath. *It isn't an emergency*, she told herself. *He's not injured or critically ill. I need to have patience. There are other people who are much sicker than my husband.*

At least that's what she told herself, and she prayed that this rationale would get her through the day. She still needed to meet with Joel and Maribelle about the store's financial situation.

✻ ✻ ✻

As soon as she finished the thought, her cell phone rang. She was comforted to hear her store manager's voice, and she greeted her warmly.

"Maribelle, I'm so glad you called. I wanted to thank you for being here for us last night. It was a blessing to have you and Joel here to calm my nerves."

"Did it really calm your nerves, Ginnie, or did what Joel said make you worry even more about Clem?"

"Well, I have to admit, that brief conversation sent my mind in a million directions, especially after you left and I persuaded Clem to go to bed. When the house was quiet, I started having thoughts that didn't get me anywhere that I needed to go. But I praise God that he was able to reach through my fretfulness and reassure me that he's with us. I managed to get a little sleep — not enough, but some."

"Ginnie, I don't know what I would do in your situation. I know you're worried about Clem — we all are — but you're handling it so well. I wish I had your faith."

"Trust me, dear, the Lord and I had to talk for a *long* time last night. It hasn't been easy."

"How is Clem today? Are things going OK?"

"It's as though nothing ever happened, Maribelle. It's the strangest thing. We didn't talk about his foray into the squirrels' domain yesterday, and I've been debating about whether to bring it up now, with just the two of us, or wait until we see the doctor. I've called Doc March's office, and they're going to let me know if they can squeeze him in today. I sure hope so. I'm trying not to worry, but you should have seen him last night, shivering on the patio but acting like nothing was wrong."

"Ginnie, what can I do to help?" Maribelle said. "I'm afraid I've been adding to your stress lately instead of making things easier for you. I'm so sorry."

"Don't be ridiculous. You've been a blessing, my dear. None of this bookkeeping business is your fault, and I want you to understand that."

"I feel so helpless, though," Maribelle said. "I wish I could wave a magic wand and make all your troubles disappear."

Ginnie laughed, and it blessed Maribelle that her employer and dear friend could still laugh under these circumstances.

"If life worked that way — if we could merely wave a wand or snap our fingers to make life go our way all the time — how would we ever realize our profound need for Jesus?" Ginnie reminded Maribelle.

Maribelle knew she was right, but that didn't mean she had to like it. A magic wand seemed like a really good option right now.

✳ ✳ ✳

When Maribelle hung up from talking to Ginnie, she texted Joel.

Maribelle: Just talked to Ginnie she said Clem's acting normal today but she's still worried

Joel: Is she taking him to the doctor?

Maribelle: They're trying to fit him in I don't think she's going to be able to meet with us today she wants to stay with him

Joel: I'll call you in a few minutes. I'm wrapping up a project with a colleague this morning but should be able to talk in an hour. That OK?

Maribelle: √

* * *

An hour later, when Maribelle saw Joel's name on the caller ID, her heart did a flip-flop.

What was *that* about — this nonsense about getting all mushy-gushy when she thought of him? She and Joel had a professional relationship, and she still wasn't sure whether he was friend or foe. After all, he hadn't cleared her — or anyone at the store, for that matter — in the mystery of the unpaid invoices.

Maribelle had to laugh at herself. She was starting to think of the bookkeeping situation in terms of the suspense novels she had been reading since she was a kid, especially those with names like "The Mysterious Affair at Styles" or "The Purloined Letter." Even Ginnie had referred to the secret stash of bills as "the mystery tin" last night, even when she was so worried about Clem. It would be hilarious if it weren't so serious.

Maribelle was afraid that if she didn't laugh, she would cry. So far, with the help of her gray-haired kitty and a box of peppermint tea roughly the size of mainland China, she had managed to hold everything together, but that didn't mean the slightest stressor wouldn't tip the scales in favor of an ugly meltdown right in the middle of the grocery store aisle — if she ever had time to go grocery shopping again.

By the fourth ring of her cell phone, Maribelle pulled herself out of her reverie and picked up.

"You busy?" Joel asked.

"Not too busy for you."

Now, why did she say that? She sounded like a moon-eyed teenager, or worse.

"Uh, I mean … I'm eager to get this bookkeeping situation settled, so I'm all yours. I mean …"

Drat. To continue would only make it worse, so she forced herself to shut up.

Joel chuckled.

"I know what you mean. I'm eager to wrap it up, too. Not that I've minded getting to know you these past few days, but I realize that this has been causing a lot of stress for you and your employers, and I want to help you reach a happy ending."

Now they were *both* starting to sound like characters in a teen romance.

"So what are you proposing?" she said.

She should have quit while she was ahead.

"Can we meet in your office? I don't think it matters that the staff will see me with you there. Once I tell you my new theory, you're bound to agree. And then we can decide on the next step."

"Come whenever you can," she told him. "There's no use in scheduling a time; the store gets busy when it gets busy. It's unpredictable this close to Christmas."

"I'll be there as soon as I can."

* * *

Joel must have hit all the green lights on the drive from his office to Bedford Books, for he arrived in a surprisingly short amount of time.

"Wow, you didn't waste any time," Maribelle said as she took his gray wool coat and purple scarf and draped them over the office filing cabinet before gesturing for Joel to sit at the desk.

"I could be completely wrong about this, Maribelle. And, to tell you the truth, I'm not sure whether I hope I'm wrong or I'm right."

"You've had me curious ever since we talked on the phone. Frankly, I'm glad you ran all the red lights in town to make it here so fast," she grinned.

"I had a police escort, so I didn't get any speeding tickets," he teased.

She was starting to get used to the way Joel's smile crinkled up his green eyes and warmed her insides, and she found herself not wanting that to end. She almost — in a crazy, irrational sort of way — wished that the bookkeeping mystery could continue so that she could keep having conversations with this extremely handsome and kind man every day.

He was growing on her; that was for sure.

She and Joel were starting to be at ease around each other. She wondered what it would be like to be his girlfriend, having relaxed conversations about their everyday lives, chatting about their work and church and things as mundane as the weather and their pets and what to cook for dinner the next evening.

And what his lips would feel like on hers.

Whoa, girl. Back it up. What was the thought just before the kissing part? Let's concentrate on that.

Did he even like to cook? It would be grand if he did. She could picture him boiling a pot of pasta on the stove, salting and testing to be sure the dish came out just the way she liked it. Seasoning vegetables to roast in the oven until they were mouthwateringly perfect. Special birthday dinners, cozy date nights, chats in front of the fireplace.

Chats that ended when he kissed her goodnight.

She caught herself for the umpteenth time. What had gotten into her? Was it the Christmas season? Was she getting ... *hopeful* again?

Well, if so, she needed to snap out of it.

Concentrate, Maribelle. Joel came to discuss the bookkeeping situation. Calm your adolescent self down and listen.

"So ... I'm almost afraid to ask," she said. "What's your theory?"

"Now that I think about it, I don't know that I can call it an actual theory. Let's call it ... just a hunch. Or maybe just an idea I'd like to run by you. I'm not even sure how the idea came to me, except that I was praying for clarity and insight, and it popped into my head."

"OK, spill the beans. I'm dying to know," Maribelle said.

"Let me start by telling you about my mother."

Joel looked into Maribelle's eyes as if he was trying to gauge whether to trust her with this tender part of his life. It was still somewhat raw, despite the passage of time. It had been a few years, but to Joel it still felt as though it had all happened last week.

Maribelle, seated in a straight-backed chair angled toward Joel in Clem's office chair, reached out and instinctively touched the back of his hand to give him strength to share what was obviously hard for him to say. Joel turned his hand over and held onto hers, still hesitating to speak.

"Joel," Maribelle said gently, looking straight into his green eyes, all the way to his soul. "You can trust me."

"I know." He paused, with a lump in his throat. "I know."

In that moment, two thoughts battled for Joel's attention: *I want to kiss her*, followed by *I want to share this part of my life with her.*

He chose the latter.

"I don't talk about this," he told her.

"You can trust me," she repeated.

He smiled, then cleared his throat and folded his arms across his chest, preparing himself to tell the story.

"My mother and I were very close. Dad was gone a lot, and my sister was several years older, so in a lot of ways I felt like an only child. My parents didn't intend for it to be that way, but they had trouble having children, and the timing of our births was just ... not in their control. Mom lost two babies between Jennifer and me."

"I'm so sorry, Joel," Maribelle murmured.

"Yeah, me, too." He smiled sadly and continued.

"By the time Mom started showing signs of dementia, Jennifer was married with a family of her own, and she and her husband had moved to Seattle to raise their children. Her husband grew up there. Sometimes I think Jenny would have moved back when Mom started getting worse, but he seemed to have laid a guilt trip on her for wanting to uproot the kids and move across the country. At the time I thought he was just being selfish, but now I don't know.

"For whatever reason, Jenny and Scott stayed in the Northwest and I stayed here to take care of our mother."

"Where was your dad?" Maribelle asked.

"Working all the time. In denial. Making excuses. Letting me bear all the burdens of taking care of her."

"Wow." It came out softly, and it was all Maribelle could think of to say. She was learning to keep her mouth shut when in doubt.

"At first, we thought Mom was just overloaded with work. We tried to get her to slow down, cut back on her hours — all the usual things you tell someone who's under stress, when you think a busy schedule is all that's wrong."

"When you say 'we' ..." Maribelle began.

"Dad was around enough to notice that something wasn't right, but, again, he just thought she was overworked, and he ignored any evidence that might indicate anything more dire. Eventually, when I realized that Mom's problem was more serious than a heavy work schedule, I moved back home. I had graduated with my accounting degree and been out on my own for a few years, but I was still living nearby — just a few miles across town. I realized that Mom needed someone around all the time, especially during her waking hours."

"What did your mom do for a living?" Maribelle prompted.

"Oh, yeah. I forgot that part. She was a registered nurse. In fact, she was the director of nursing at Harbor Medical Center for many years. No stress there, right?" he smiled wryly.

Joel had mentioned his mother once before, in a brief conversation about their childhood years while they waited for their food at Difalso's, but she hadn't asked him whether his parents were still living.

When Joel had told Ginnie the evening before, "She had Alzheimer's disease," Maribelle had gotten her answer — at least about his mom. When someone mentions Alzheimer's in the past tense, there is really no other conclusion to draw. To Maribelle's knowledge, no one had ever survived Alzheimer's. It was a relentlessly cruel disease that left sorrow, pain and a sense of helplessness in its wake.

"Joel, I think I know where you're going with this," Maribelle said, touching the back of his hand again.

He had been looking past her as he told his mother's story, but at Maribelle's gentle words he looked straight at her, into her eyes. Her pale blue eyes were kind, he seemed to notice for the first time.

"You think Clem is in the early stages of dementia, don't you?" she said matter-of-factly.

"I think it's possible. I mean, until recently I hadn't seen the Hatches since I was a kid, so obviously I don't know them that well. But then you told me his reaction to the broken Santa Claus and the fact that, at a retailer's busiest time of the year, Clem had been staying home the past several days instead of coming to the store — a business that's been his heart and soul for decades. It got me to thinking about the invoices and the secret tin hidden behind the files, and things started fitting together in my mind."

Now it was Joel's turn to speak in a rush of thoughts and an overflow of words.

"Now, I could be completely off base — and, like I said, I'm not sure whether to hope I'm right or hope I'm wrong — but I think we should investigate this possibility. We've reached no plausible answers on the hidden invoices, and I've seen this type of behavior firsthand."

"Should we tell Ginnie?"

"No!" Joel regretted the force with which the word came out of his mouth.

"Sorry, I didn't mean to be so abrupt. And it may be too late; I've already mentioned Alzheimer's to Ginnie, and I regret that somewhat. Let's see what Clem's doctor has to say, and meanwhile you and I can test our theory."

Joel corrected himself: "My theory, I mean."

"*Our* theory," Maribelle said. "We're in this together."

She smiled at him, and he felt like wrapping his arms around her in gratitude … and maybe a few other emotions.

"Whatever you think we should do, Joel, I'll follow your lead."

"We're partners, Ms. Reed," Joel said with a smile. "This will require us to put our heads together and work as a team.

"I need you," he said, looking her straight in the eye.

Maribelle wouldn't have been able to put words to the swirling tornado in her heart if her life depended on it.

And maybe Clem's life did.

18

Maribelle sat across from Joel in the same booth they had shared the first time they dined at Difalso's.

Tonight it was different, though.

Different objectives, different game plan ... different ambience.

... Budding and unfamiliar emotions.

Joel's earlier assumptions about the candlelight had been on the mark. Tonight the house lights were dimmer, and candles flickered on all the tables, turning each private alcove hopelessly romantic by the mere presence of the glowing red-beaded holders accenting the white tablecloths. The small booth in the back corner was cozier tonight than when he had first sat down to dine with the pretty bookstore manager, even though the "less-stressful circumstances" he had envisioned were still on the horizon.

He hoped.

He wanted to bring Maribelle here again someday soon, when the invoice mystery was solved, when Clem's Alzheimer's scare was merely a funny story — an unfortunate miscalculation of the stress he and Ginnie had truly been under.

Oh, how Joel wanted to be wrong. In the beginning, he wanted to be wrong about an embezzler in the store's midst. Now, he actually wanted that to be true. He wanted so desperately for there to be a thief of the store's money, but not of his friend Clem's sound and generous mind. After not hearing from Ginnie all day, Maribelle had checked in with her in the late afternoon. The doctor wasn't going to be able to see Clem today, but the receptionist promised to fit him in first thing the next morning. That was a relief, but it would be another night of concern, in which they all tried not to jump to conclusions and let worry rob them of the restorative sleep each one of them needed.

As Joel sat across the table from this woman he was beginning to grow so fond of, he sat back and took a few slow breaths.

Instead of a crisp white dress shirt and a purple tie, or a lavender dress shirt and a navy tie, tonight Joel was wearing a stylishly dark purple shirt with dark gray slacks and gray socks with a hint of purple pinstripe. His gray suede Oxfords completed the semi-casual look that told Maribelle he was trying to relax despite all the problems on his mind.

"Joel," Maribelle said. "I know we came here to talk about the store and about Clem's health, but there's something I've been dying to know."

"Mmm?" he responded, as though he already had a mouthful of Italian bread.

"Has purple always been your favorite color?"

Good thing he wasn't chewing on food. He might have choked.

Joel looked at Maribelle for a moment with an inscrutable expression. He supposed they needed to have this conversation. He had already opened his heart about his mother when he and Maribelle were in the bookstore this morning. Granted, she didn't know his mother's entire story, but he had decided that he trusted her enough to share it … eventually.

He supposed he might as well start now.

"Actually," Joel began, "I've always hated purple."

Maribelle's eyebrows shot up, and she paused in the middle of a sip of ice water.

"Come again?" she said.

"You heard me right. I hate purple."

"You coulda fooled me. And about a half-dozen other people at Bedford Books."

"I know, I know. Most people assume it's my favorite color, but there's a reason I wear it … and a reason I hate it."

"I'm all ears," his dinner companion said. She placed her linen napkin next to the bread basket and leaned forward, forearms on the table.

"I'm not really sure where to start, because I have a feeling we'd be here all night if I started at the beginning. But I feel the need to come clean with you. I've begun to view you as a friend, Maribelle, and I know I can trust you with the parts of myself that I share with very few people."

"I feel the same way," she said, her beautiful blue eyes full of emotion.

He looked into those pale blue eyes for a long moment, sighed, and began.

"Maybe it's too strong a word to say I've always *hated* purple, but it was never one of my favorite colors. I never thought it looked good on me, and I never liked it on other people. Furniture, decorations, bicycles, you name it … I just didn't care for it.

"I didn't exactly have an aversion to it … until my mom got sick."

He sat back in his seat and closed his eyes, the pain of so many emotionally draining years evident on his face.

"Have you ever been around someone whose mind has been stolen from them?" he asked Maribelle. "Someone you used to idolize, who was brilliant and kind and funny and nurturing, and who could make the best peanut butter and jelly sandwich on the planet?"

"Your mom sounds like an amazing woman," Maribelle said.

"She was, and not just because she was my mom. She graduated top of her class in nursing school and won all kinds of accolades in her school years and later in her nursing career. Mom originally wanted to earn a medical degree but sacrificed her own plans so that my dad could realize his. That happens so much with women, even today. I would never ask my wife to give up her dreams the way my father allowed my mother to do for him."

"But I bet that if you asked her," Maribelle said, "she would voice no regrets about having you and your sister and bringing up her family the way she did. Would she?"

"No, you're right," Joel said. "Even if she had regrets, she would never admit them to us. But she would have made a brilliant doctor. Who knows what she might have accomplished if she'd just had the chance."

"Joel, you can't regret her choices for her. She chose her family over being a physician. And nursing is just as noble a profession as doctoring. In fact, I much prefer a lot of the nurses I've dealt with to some of the doctors I've had experience with over the years."

Joel smiled.

"I realize that sounds condescending to the nursing profession. I hate stereotypes, and I agree that nursing and 'medicine' are equally noble career choices. But Mom wanted to be a doctor, and she gave up that opportunity."

"Willingly, though, right?"

"If you call emotional blackmail by your spouse being a *willing* participant," he said.

Maribelle let that one go. Joel could tell her that story in his own time if he chose to. It was obviously a raw subject for him.

"So how does the color purple fit into that story?" she prompted.

"Mom actually loved purple, and I had no specific problem with it, except that it just wasn't one of my favorite colors, as I said."

"Do you wear it in her memory?"

"Well, hers and the millions of other people with Alzheimer's disease. Did you know that purple is the official color of the Alzheimer's Association?"

"I guess I hadn't paid much attention, but I do remember seeing certain celebrities wearing purple during Alzheimer's Awareness Month, now that you mention it," Maribelle said. "So you started wearing it after she ..." Maribelle wasn't sure whether to continue. Either Joel started wearing purple every day when his mother was in the throes of the devastating illness ... or when she died. Either way, she didn't think she needed to finish the sentence.

"When it was obvious we couldn't count on my father to step up and be a man — to take his turn at sacrificing for the woman who gave up so much for him — that's when I moved back home," Joel continued. "In my spare time, before I had to watch Mom pretty much around the clock, I started relentlessly researching dementia, especially Alzheimer's disease. I made the association's website the home page on my internet browser, and every morning I saw purple when I logged on.

"Purple followed me everywhere. It even started invading my dreams. At the time, I wasn't getting enough sleep, and when I did, it was tortured. It was like a strange vortex of purple, red and black that sucked me in every time I tried to get a few minutes of rest. Even when I managed to sleep, I couldn't escape the horror of my mother's illness or do anything to save her from its cruelty.

"I felt so helpless."

Joel closed his eyes again, and Maribelle reached out and stroked the back of his hand with her fingertips.

"I understand that most caregivers have a sense of helplessness, to varying degrees," she said. "I'm so sorry, Joel. It must have been awful."

"There's no way for me to describe how awful it was," he said. "Maybe someday I'll try, but I don't want to spoil your dinner. Besides, we came here to talk about ways we can help Clem. He's still with us, praise God, and he has the more immediate need."

"Joel, I've been trying to practice gratitude every day this month because of my previously crummy attitude — and I do mean *crummy* attitude. I feel as though I've taken so many things for granted lately," Maribelle said. "Would it be OK if we paused for a moment so I can say a prayer?"

"Maribelle, I'm so sorry I didn't start our dinner that way," Joel said. "I guess I'm just as stressed out and distracted as you and your employers are. Which just means prayer should have been our first action!"

"It's OK. You're right; it's so easy to forget how important prayer is when you're in the thick of a difficult situation."

"Do you want me to pray?" Joel asked Maribelle.

"Actually, I'd like to, if you don't mind."

He took her hand in his and bowed his head.

"Dear heavenly Father," she began. "So many times we get so caught up in our struggles that we forget to thank you for what's right in front of our faces. I want to thank you tonight for bringing Joel into my life."

Joel opened his eyes and stole a quiet glance at this young woman who was beginning to steal his heart. Etched on her face he saw a sincerity and wisdom that he hadn't noticed before. Had it been missing until this moment, or had he simply failed to realize how wise this beautiful woman of God was?

He also realized that he, himself, had many things to be grateful for, including grace. Not only God's grace for him and for all mankind, but for the grace that Maribelle had been showing him amid extremely trying circumstances.

Maribelle had confided to him how difficult her first year as store manager had been, but then there was the business with the invoices — which would be enough to send anyone lurching for the peppermint tea (well, most people, if not him) — and finally the uncertainty of Clem's situation. Lord only knew what other burdens she was carrying that she hadn't shared with him.

The beautiful woman sitting across the flickering candlelight from him had strength that Joel had failed to appreciate until this very moment.

Maribelle continued her prayer.

"Lord, thank you for Clem and Ginnie, for modern medicine, for doctors *and* nurses, and for how Joel has entrusted me with the story of his mother. Help me remember each day to thank you for my blessings. And most of all, thank you for the gift of your Son, Jesus Christ, who died for my sins and the sins of the whole world. It's in His precious name I pray, amen."

"Amen," Joel murmured as he squeezed Maribelle's hand.

She looked up at him and smiled, and his heart skipped a beat.

"I didn't quite finish the story about my love-hate relationship with purple, but I'd like to table it for now, if you don't mind. Let's talk about Clem, and then maybe we can talk about something completely unrelated and happy while we indulge in some dessert."

"You're speaking my language, pal," Maribelle said with a grin. "Difalso's tiramisu was sent down from heaven by angels on a special assignment from God. And their double-dark-chocolate flourless cake will make your eyes roll back in your head."

"Wow. They both sound great — and rich. Maybe we could split one of them; I'll let you pick."

"Nothin' doin'. If I order that chocolate cake, you'll come away with fork marks in the back of your hand if you try to steal a bite."

"Duly warned," Joel said, but her smile told him he'd probably get away with it if he took the risk.

19

"Joel, come quickly!" Maribelle shouted from the office doorway.

Joel had stopped at the back door to tie his shoelace when he heard the urgent shout from his co-conspirator.

The duo had gone straight to the bookstore from the Italian restaurant and, after unlocking the alley door, Maribelle had gone inside first to turn on the lights and bump up the thermostat. At the moment she shouted, a flash of panic coursed through Joel, and he wished she had let him enter the dark building first. After all, they still weren't 100 percent certain that they didn't have a criminal in their midst; Joel's theory, while plausible, was still just a theory. In the short time they had known each other, Joel had grown somewhat protective of Maribelle, and he didn't want to fail her now.

He raced in, nearly tripping over a delivery box half-full of books.

"What is it?" he said as he skidded to a stop in front of Maribelle.

She turned around and pointed, her face white.

Sitting in the middle of Clem's desk was a smiling Santa Claus: ceramic, old-fashioned, jolly — and, tonight, just a little creepy — who bore a striking resemblance to the one Maribelle had shattered into a million pieces last week.

"What is it?" Joel repeated, calmer this time. He had looked around the room but didn't notice anything to be concerned about.

"Santa," she said, barely opening her mouth.

"Yeah ...?" His tone and his pause indicated that it was a question, but Maribelle didn't bite, so he asked it more straightforwardly: "Are you afraid of Santa Claus?"

"In general, no. But *this* Santa Claus, yes. That looks exactly like the ceramic Santa that I broke. You know, the antique one that belonged to Clem's grandmother."

"Well, obviously it's not the same one," Joel said, to Maribelle's extreme annoyance.

"I know that," she said a little more curtly than she intended. "But where did it come from? How did it get here? Who's been in this office since I left this afternoon?"

"Is there a note with it?" he said, stepping around Maribelle and walking toward the desk. He caught a whiff of garlic on her breath and smiled as he thought of their cozy dinner.

Joel looked around and didn't see anything out of the ordinary. He picked up Santa and looked underneath. No note on the desk under the fat man. He turned him over. The inscription on the flat bottom that was painted into the ceramic was light gray and a bit fuzzy, too faint to make out, making Joel think this Santa was an older model, just like the one Maribelle had broken.

Another mystery.

"Is there a box?" he asked, taking another panoramic look around the small office.

"Only those boxes that have been sitting there for a month," Maribelle said. "There's nothing in them but a bunch of older books we're saving for an after-Christmas sale. And I'm pretty sure this dude wasn't hiding in one of them, just waiting for his twin brother to bite the dust so he could come crawling out to give me the heebie-jeebies. He looks just like the first Santa."

"Well, there's got to be a logical explanation for it," Joel said, hoping he was right. "Shattered Santas don't just come back from the dead. Unless ..."

"Unless what?" Maribelle said, eyeing him suspiciously.

"Unless he's the Ghost of Christmas Past!"

She socked him in the arm with her elbow, having no clue that he had a big sutured gash in that arm.

"Ow!" Joel grabbed his wounded arm with his left hand.

"Oh, I didn't hit you that hard," Maribelle said. "Don't be so melodramatic."

"Who's calling whom melodramatic?" he said. "Ceramic Santas coming back from the dead?"

She glared at him.

"And, to tell the truth," Joel said, "my arm actually is injured. I was in the emergency room recently for stitches after an accident at work."

"Really?" She gasped in horror at her own insensitivity. "I'm so sorry, Joel. I had no idea. Why didn't you tell me?"

"I didn't think it was any big deal — until now." He grinned at

Maribelle, his expression half "it's OK" and half "I'm a he-man who can handle anything."

She wasn't buying any of it.

"Joel, I feel so bad ..." she began. "... But wait a second. You said you injured your arm at work? What kind of accounting firm do you work for, anyway? Do they give you hazard pay?"

He laughed. "No, but maybe I should ask for some," he joked.

"I didn't mean to keep it a secret," he said. "With everything going on, I hadn't thought to mention it. I tripped over something in my office and fell onto a glass table, which shattered. I did need stitches, but I'm a pretty fast healer, so it doesn't bother me much — until a beautiful woman socks me in the exact spot where it hurts!"

Did Joel just say she was beautiful? Maribelle tried to shake the idea out of her head. He was probably just trying to lighten the mood so she wouldn't feel guilty about punching his injured arm.

She wanted to ask more about the accident but decided to drop the subject. After all, they had come here to do some detective work. Detective work that wasn't supposed to include creepy ceramic Santas. But Joel *had* called her a "beautiful woman." She blushed, savoring the warmth of those words, as much as she tried to shift gears and focus.

Santa Claus still sat and stared at them.

"Santa, I swept you into the garbage. What are you doing back?"

"Mare," Joel said. "It's not the same Santa. There's no way. From what you told me, he was in too many pieces to put back together. Don't you think we'd be able to tell if someone glued him? And what about his skinned nose? This Santa's nose is perfectly ... jolly."

"The logical side of my brain says you're right," Maribelle replied. "But it creeps me out, anyway. I need a cup of tea."

Drat! Joel thought. Maybe she'd wait until he took her home to have the tea. That way he wouldn't have to inhale the fumes.

"Do you think I should call the staff and ask for an explanation?" Maribelle said as she dug around in the desk for her tin of peppermint tea.

"Let them rest, Maribelle. They have their own lives, and there's no use stirring everyone up this evening. It's only a Santa statue."

"I know; you're right. But I'm not sure *I'm* going to be able to rest," she sighed. "This is just weird, and maybe I'm too exhausted to make any sense, but tonight I'm putting Santa on my naughty list. Until I have an explanation for how he got here, he's going in a box with a lid as soon as I find one, even if I have to empty out an order of books."

"I'll help you find a box," Joel said. She seemed to have forgotten about the peppermint tea, so he was willing to do anything to keep her mind off of it until he got her home.

* * *

Joel still hadn't explained his reason for wanting to be in the store to test his theory about Clem and the bookkeeping situation.

"What are we looking for?" Maribelle asked as they sat at the desk after placing Mr. Ho Ho Ho inside a box and then onto a high shelf in the storage room.

"Anything out of the ordinary for Clem," Joel said. "Anything you may not have had a second thought about before, but maybe now, with fresh eyes, you see it in a different light."

"I wish my eyes were fresh tonight, but at this point all I want to do is go home and curl up with my cat and a hot cup of tea."

Peppermint, no doubt, Joel thought as he tried not to grimace.

"You're right, Maribelle. I'm sorry. We should take this up again tomorrow."

"Joel, I haven't asked you this before, but how are you able to spend this much time away from your office?" Maribelle said. He had been spending several hours a day working on the Bedford Books case, and now he was fretting about Clem's mental state, too — although she supposed the two might be inextricably bound.

"I was wrapping up a project right about the time Clem called me, and he and Ginnie *are* paying my firm for my auditing services, after all. But on the days I'm not actively working on the audit for the bookstore, I'm using vacation time."

"What?" Maribelle gasped. "You're using your vacation time for Clem and Ginnie?"

This man was even more generous than she had realized. He had to have some ancient skeleton in his closet; he was just too perfect.

"I'm doing it for you, too, Maribelle."

She blushed.

"But why? Why would you go out of your way to help me?"

Joel looked at Maribelle.

"Because."

"Because ..." she prompted.

"Well, at first I was here because Clem asked for my help, and I remembered him as a kind man when I was a boy. I wanted to help him and Ginnie figure out what was going on so they could keep their store in business. They're good people. Also, I like to solve puzzles, and this seemed like a way to keep myself occupied while I was supposed to be on 'light duty' after my accident, especially since we wind down a bit in December. And then it was because ..."

"What, Joel?" Maribelle said, nudging him to spill it.

"Because I don't think you did anything wrong. And ..."

He was just going to say it.

"Because I think you're wonderful."

Maribelle didn't think she'd need that peppermint tea now.

✶ ✶ ✶

Had she heard Joel correctly?

Did he just say she was wonderful?

"Joel, could you repeat that?" she said softly. She was almost afraid to ask, but she wanted to hear it again, to make sure she hadn't dreamed it. And, if she hadn't dreamed it, she wanted to savor it.

He looked into her eyes and smiled.

"I think you're wonderful."

Maribelle's fair skin turned pink, her pale blue eyes misted over and her heart did a couple of somersaults.

"No one's ever said that to me before," she confessed.

"I find that hard to believe," Joel said. "A woman like you ... smart, compassionate, beautiful ..."

"Do you really think I'm beautiful?" The dream just kept getting better.

"I do. I've been trying to ignore my attraction to you, but it's been getting more and more difficult. And when you prayed at the restaurant tonight ... when you thanked God for me, well, that pretty much sealed it for me. I knew I had to tell you how I felt. I never thought I would meet a woman who loves God as much as I do, and wants to include him in every aspect of her life. But now I have. There are no words for how incredible that makes me feel. So, yes, I think you're pretty wonderful."

And suddenly Maribelle felt completely safe.

Safe, cherished, warm.

Calm.

Joel thought she was wonderful, and he loved that she was a woman of God.

This wasn't a dream. (If it had been a dream, she wouldn't be a dozen pounds overweight and chocolate would be an official food group, but one that had zero calories.)

When Maribelle looked up at Joel, her eyes were brimming with tears.

"Joel … thank you."

Before she could say any more, she needed to take a few deep breaths … and say a prayer of thanks.

She closed her eyes and silently said a quick prayer, then looked up again.

"But I'm afraid to say how I feel," she started.

"You can trust me, Maribelle."

"I think I can, but I've been hurt badly, and I'm not sure I know how to trust anyone."

Joel took her hand and caressed the tops of her fingers with his thumb, sending a thrill through Maribelle.

"Once the words are out there, Joel, I can't take them back."

"Sometimes you just have to take a risk, Maribelle," he said softly, looking into her eyes. His hand went to her face, and his thumb traced her cheekbone. He let it linger there for a moment, then pushed a stray ringlet of hair behind her ear, where she normally tried to keep it.

His touch was so gentle and loving, Maribelle wanted to say the words.

I love you, Joel.

But she couldn't.

It had been nearly two years since her fiancé had broken her heart, but in some ways it was like it had happened yesterday. The pain was still fresh. She hadn't moved on.

"Joel, I need to do some work on myself. I realized at this moment that I've been letting myself remain stuck in the past. I think it's why Christmas has lost its joy for me. You've helped me realize that. I need to get my joy back, and I need to move on from the hurts I've been reliving for two years."

"Did something specific cause you to be hurt?" He didn't want to pry, but he wanted — no, *needed* — to know.

"I was engaged to be married, and it didn't work out," she said, avoiding Joel's eyes. "Let's leave it at that for now. I think I'll be able to talk to you about it eventually, but I need to work it out for myself first. Is that OK?"

"Of course it's OK, Maribelle. I understand, and I'll be here when you're ready."

Again, his words nearly brought her to tears.

This wonderful man. Why couldn't she trust him?

Maribelle had a lot of work to do.

* * *

As Joel drove her home, Maribelle fretted about Dickens. Her old rescue animal was getting up in years — at least for a cat — and Maribelle had been concerned about his health. He was slowing down, she confided to Joel, and it made her sad.

Then it occurred to her: She had never asked Joel about his home life.

"Do you have any pets?" she asked as a gentle snow tickled the windshield in the dark.

"Yup. Me and old Shirley go way back."

"Shirley?"

Joel chuckled, then launched into the story.

"Several years ago, I was helping a recently divorced woman sort through her taxable assets after her husband abandoned her for a younger woman."

"Oh, how awful!" Maribelle exclaimed.

"Yeah, it was," he said. "I really felt sorry for her. I mean, she was rich, but money can't cure the kind of heartbreak this woman went through because of her husband's selfishness."

He continued his tale, trying not to get sidetracked with thoughts of his father's treatment of his mother.

"Just before he left her, when she didn't have a clue what was about to happen — and apparently he hadn't decided to leave yet — the husband had bought a puppy, whom he had named Samson. And whom his wife hated."

"The wife — let's call her Mrs. Smith — had been against the purchase and wanted nothing to do with Samson. When her husband left, his new girlfriend wouldn't have the puppy, so Mr. Smith left him with my client.

"The first time I visited Mrs. Smith's house on business, Samson climbed onto my lap on the sofa and rolled over for a belly rub. I looked down for a minute, then said to Mrs. Smith, 'Did you say your dog's name was Samson?'

"Mrs. Smith replied coldly, 'First of all, he's not my dog. He's *his* dog. Secondly, yes, that is his name.'

"Ma'am, I think you might want to reconsider that name," I told her. "This dog is ... a female."

Maribelle snorted.

"Sorry," she said. "I know it's not funny, but ... it sort of is."

"You're right," Joel told Maribelle. "It *is* funny, and it's OK to laugh. ... So I say to her, 'The dog is a female,' and Mrs. Smith says indignantly, 'Oh? I hadn't noticed.'

"*Obviously*," Joel said to Maribelle. "Then she said, 'Well, it matters not. I'm not keeping him.'

" 'What are you going to do with her?' I asked Mrs. Smith, emphasizing the *her*. 'I'm going to have him destroyed,' she said coldly.

"I grabbed her arm before I could stop myself. 'Ma'am, no! You can't do that!' I said, probably a little more forcefully than I should have. After all, she was a client and I barely knew her.

"She looked at me and said haughtily, 'Well, *surely* you don't expect me to keep him ... er, her. Every day since my husband left, that dog is a reminder of how he betrayed me. I won't have it around.'

" 'Don't you know someone who could take her?' I asked Mrs. Smith.

"None of my friends would have her. They're too loyal to me. Besides, even then I'd surely be reminded of *him* every time I visited with my friends. No. It's too much to ask."

" 'But Mrs. Smith, you can't destroy the dog just because your husband was cruel to you,' I told her. 'That would be cruel to Samson. I think the dog might become a good companion for you if you gave her half a chance.'

" 'Surely you aren't serious,' Mrs. Smith said to me.

"And by the time I left her house that day, I was the proud owner of a bulldog named Shirley with a purple rhinestone collar and a raincoat."

Maribelle was almost beside herself with laughter.

"OK, first of all, Mrs. Smith was never going to destroy that dog," she said. "If a woman hates a dog, she doesn't buy it raincoats and rhinestone collars — and she *surely* doesn't let it climb up on her fancy furniture. I think the Lord just knew you needed Shirley more than Mrs. Smith did."

"Hmm. Maybe," Joel said. "So, what else? I know there's a Part 2 coming."

"I'm pretty *sure* I know why you named her Shirley." Maribelle sat back in her seat, pretty pleased with herself.

Joel laughed heartily. "My friend, *surely* you are a good detective!"

20

The next morning, Joel texted Maribelle before she left the house:

Joel: Can we do some more detective work this morning? I'm eager to wrap up our investigation before Christmas.

Maribelle: Good morning to you too Joel how's Shirley

Joel: She's doing fine, Mare. She surely is. ☺

Maribelle: Funny. ☺ I can meet you at the office at 7:00. That OK?

Joel: Works for me. See you then.

Maribelle had trouble brushing her teeth because she couldn't wipe the smile off her face. She and Joel were growing closer, starting to share personal stories and inside jokes, texting each other about things outside their original purpose for being in contact — solving the accounting mystery — and generally enjoying each other's company. Last night he had texted her a meme depicting a bulldog in a pink tutu that he had seen on the internet. Maribelle went to bed with a smile on her face, Dickens purring gently at her feet.

Yes, life was taking a pleasant upturn, at least in the relationship department. It didn't mean life was candy canes and dancing elves, though. Matters with Clem were still worrisome, they still hadn't solved the accounting mystery and she still had yet to start writing her Great American Novel — but Maribelle's personal life was definitely looking up.

It couldn't last, she told herself the next minute as the cynicism flared up again. She had never been that lucky. Not that she believed in luck, but if it did exist she usually didn't have any of the good kind.

Gloom, despair and agony threatened to extinguish the buzz that Joel had brought to her mood with his two most recent text messages.

Maribelle chided herself. She knew she needed to nip that line of thinking right in the bud. How easily those nasty thoughts could bloom, though. The depression she had experienced after her breakup could come barreling back if she didn't keep herself grounded in the truth of God's love for her and his purpose for her life.

She looked herself in the eye for a long moment in the mirror, rinsed the toothpaste drool off her chin and went back to her bed. She climbed on top of the covers and reached for her Bible on the nightstand. She had skipped writing her gratitude list yesterday, so she grabbed her notebook and pen, sat back and opened to the Psalms.

But let all who take refuge in you rejoice;
let them sing joyful praises forever.
Spread your protection over them,
that all who love your name may be filled with joy.
For you bless the godly, O Lord;
you surround them with your shield of love.

Maribelle hadn't noticed this section of Psalms before — at least in any meaningful way. Today it had special meaning, not only for herself but for everyone she loved. She thought of Clem and Ginnie, of Bethany, Todd and Adam at the store, of her family … and of Joel.

She prayed the two verses from Psalm 5 over each of them.

She prayed that the Lord would spread his protection over each of them and surround them with his shield of love. And she prayed that they would realize these blessings in very tangible ways.

"Lord give us answers today, please," she pleaded. "And help me love my people well, no matter what happens."

* * *

While Maribelle was curled up with her Bible and Dickens on the patchwork quilt in her bedroom, Joel was on his knees at the foot of his queen-size bed.

"Lord, we need answers. You know everything that's going on and everything that's about to happen in and around us. I can't help feeling you're about to reveal some things to us today. But even if that's not true, I pray that we trust you, because we know that you want only the best for us. Help us understand what you want us to do. Help me support those around me, and help us to love each other well, especially if things are going to get tougher instead of easier. We know that you're with us *always*, even in the hard times. Help us remember that. Thank you, Father, for how you love us."

✳ ✳ ✳

Maribelle already had the thermostat turned up and the teapot on by the time Joel arrived at the alleyway door of Bedford Books.

A light snow had been falling since dawn, and the winter sun was competing for air space so it could show off. The intermittent peeks of brilliant sunshine turned everything in the area to sparkling crystal and shimmering pearl for brief, stunning moments. Again today, Maribelle was convinced she could smell the snow. It was such a part of her history.

So many memories flooded back when she thought of the fragrance of Christmas.

One of her favorite holiday scents was pine. Her family had always cut down a live tree at Christmastime; her dad was so sentimental.

Matthew Reed loved to tell the story of Maribelle's birth. Invariably, he would get a dreamy look in his eyes when he began the tale. He would tell it to anyone willing to listen, but his favorite audience of one was his baby girl, Maribelle. Daddy's sweet little curly-haired Maribelle, born on Christmas morning, just after midnight, during a snowstorm.

Matt barely got his young wife to the hospital in time.

The baby's due date wasn't until Jan. 3, but because babies tend to appear when they're ready to appear, Maribelle's parents were blessed with a Dec. 25 baby. Because of the special day she decided to make her debut, her parents switched gears on the name.

Matt, being crazy for Christmas (not to mention wild for his new daughter), decided that Belle would be a perfect name. Christina, being ever the practical one, preferred a more prosaic name: Mary. Because both names were fitting for a Dec. 25 birth, their brand new baby girl was introduced to the world as Maribelle, no middle name. Christina said that with practically two names already, their daughter wouldn't need the extra baggage.

Maribelle's personality in the early years was a reflection of her dad's; he was the dreamer, the writer, the poet. Mother's efforts to instill practical wisdom in their daughter caused all-out battles through the tween and teen years. By the time Maribelle had become engaged to be married, then unengaged, she supposed she reflected both parents' best and worst qualities in equal measure.

She was grateful, though — especially today, as she paused to allow her mind to treasure the sweetest memories — that Mom and Dad at least agreed on Christmas. Maribelle may have grown indifferent to the magic of the season, but she couldn't blame her parents for that. Dad always made sure the joy and wonder and magic were there, and Mom grounded their daughter in the truth of their faith. Christina always reminded Maribelle that the true reason for celebration was Jesus' birth. He had come to rescue a lost and hurting world, and Maribelle was responsible for carrying on the story.

One of the reasons Mare had wanted to be a writer was to tell the world of its need for Jesus. It's how she was best able to communicate, and she was dying to tell her stories in ways that merged her need to create with the world's desire to consume great tales.

As Joel stomped the snow off his shoes at the back door, Maribelle greeted him with a bright smile. Joel knew that his new friend was tired — he could see it in her eyes — but she seemed to have a fresh joy this morning.

What he didn't realize was that the joy was only minutes old. Maribelle had decided just before his arrival that it was time for a new beginning.

New attitude, new trust in people (and the Lord), new way of interacting with her surroundings.

No need to wait for the new year to make resolutions. Maribelle's reboot would start ... NOW.

She wanted to throw her arms around Joel when she opened the door to him, but she still felt somewhat awkward, timid, around him. She supposed it was because he was gorgeous, and, in her previous life, gorgeous had meant trouble for her. Maribelle's fiancé had been incredibly handsome, but that situation hadn't turned out well, so she couldn't trust her judgment.

She couldn't judge a book by its cover — at least when it came to men.

Besides, she had known Joel for less than a month, and that was certainly not long enough to judge someone's true intentions. Any time she was tempted to let down her guard with this kind and handsome man, she reminded herself of her disastrous previous relationship.

Nope. Better to be cautious.

But this morning it was harder than ever to keep from throwing caution to the wind and wrapping her arms around this intensely beautiful man.

Instead, she offered him coffee.

"I have the tea on for myself, but I've noticed that you don't seem to drink tea," she said. "Shall I put on a pot of coffee for you?"

"If you'll show me to the coffeepot, I can put it on. You don't have to wait on me," Joel replied. Unspoken was Joel's memory of how his mother waited on his father hand and foot most of her life, and how it had gone largely unnoticed by his dad.

"It's no trouble, but if you want to make it, at least you'll know it's done the way you like it. I'd probably mess it up!" Maribelle said.

"I'm not a coffee snob, but I do have a certain way I like to make mine, when circumstances allow. Just point me to the supplies, and I'll get 'er done."

Maribelle led him to the break room and pointed to the coffee and the pot, which had gone neglected since the last time Clem had been in. At the store, Ginnie was a tea drinker, too, and the part-time employees brought their own specialty drinks from the coffee shop a few doors down on Bailey Street.

When Maribelle was satisfied that Joel had everything he needed for his just-right pot of coffee, she headed for the storage room. She tiptoed in — she wasn't sure why — and immediately looked to the top shelf to reassure herself that she hadn't dreamed up the new Santa, and that he was still sitting high on the shelf.

He was.

Next, the office.

Maribelle was so tired and distracted, she had lost track of exactly what she was supposed to be keeping track of, accounting-wise. She realized she needed Joel.

No, she *really* needed Joel. She had come to depend on him in so many ways already. He had shown himself capable of handling financial matters, personal matters and, on some level, health matters for Bedford Books' owners. They would surely have a void when his job was finished and everyone went back to their normal lives.

But what was normal? Was Clem really ill? What if his problem wasn't dementia? What if it was a brain tumor?

Which was worse?

Wouldn't it be wonderful if the doctor found no real illness in Clem? Maybe he was just under too much strain with the workload at the store during the holidays, the stress of the financial investigation, the normal consequences of aging ... and an innocuous infection that caused temporary memory problems?

Well, now Maribelle was just dreaming up scenarios. She wasn't a doctor (or a nurse), and none of her thinking was based in reality. Joel had been the first to suspect something like dementia. She just hoped so, so badly that he was wrong.

"Are any of these coffee mugs spoken for, Mare?" Joel called from the break room. "I don't want to take someone's special mug if anyone would be averse to sharing."

"Take any of them. Clem's the only one who drinks coffee, and Ginnie's tea mug has her name on it. She wouldn't mind if you used it, though. Just whichever one you'd prefer."

Did coffee cause dementia? Had she read that somewhere? Would hot tea help cure it? She was pretty sure hot peppermint tea would cure just about anything, but Alzheimer's was probably not one of them.

There she went again, diagnosing and curing ailments she wasn't even sure were Clem's problem.

While Joel tinkered in the break room, Maribelle booted up the computer.

She decided to empty the computer's trashcan. After all, fresh start today. Might as well clean up the computer, too.

She always liked to look at the trashcan's contents before confirming that she wanted to delete. When she double-clicked the icon and opened the trash folder, she sat slack-jawed at what she saw there.

"Joel, come here!" she shouted.

He was there in a flash.

"What now?"

"The bank statements! They were in the trash can!"

"What? How did you get them back?" he demanded.

"I didn't really get them back. I guess they were never gone," she said. "Somehow they got dragged to the trash but never deleted permanently."

Joel eyed her with skepticism.

"Joel, really, it's true!"

For the first time since he met Maribelle, a huge wave of doubt about her innocence flooded through Joel.

This was awfully convenient. He stopped himself from voicing those words, but they were on the tip of his tongue.

"Why didn't you notice that before?" he asked, still with the squint-eyed look he had given her upon hearing of her "discovery." After all, Maribelle had been the one to "discover" the tin full of unpaid bills. Maybe he had let her beauty and friendliness cloud his judgment.

He usually could read people well, but his circumstances lately had been causing him to lose sleep. And maybe the medication he had been given in the emergency room had caused some latent side-effects that impaired his judgment. Maybe he couldn't trust his instincts now.

He'd have to start relying strictly on logic.

Maribelle sat there with a stricken look on her face. She was hurt to the core that Joel didn't seem to believe her.

"Joel, you're making me nervous. What are you thinking?"

"I'm trying not to say what I'm thinking, because I don't want to hurt your feelings. But the Hatches hired me to find out what's going on with the store's financial records. I have to say, Maribelle, that this 'discovery' looks awfully convenient. Why didn't you 'find' these bank records when I first requested them? You sure kept putting me off when I asked about them repeatedly."

Tears welled up in Maribelle's eyes.

"This is *exactly* what I knew would happen!" she shouted. "I knew you would suspect me! In fact, before I even met you, I knew that whatever became of my disclosure of the metal tin full of papers, I would be suspected of *something* by *someone*. That's just the way life works. It doesn't pay to be honest. Somebody's going to suspect you of something, no matter how perfectly you try to live your life."

"I'm sorry you feel that way, Maribelle. I think you're just feeling sorry for yourself now. If you're innocent, I'll find that out, but right now you just sound like a petulant child who's trying to divert attention from the real issue by garnering sympathy."

"You haven't figured it out yet! What makes you think you'll find out what's really going on if you haven't done it by now?" She was shouting louder now, trying not to spit as she yelled the words. But she was mad enough to spit nails.

"You're not even being logical, Maribelle." Logic was his new watchword, since he had decided he couldn't rely on his gut. "I haven't been given all the information I've needed to figure it out. So far I've been relying on my goodwill to keep you out of jail — or, at the very least, out of the unemployment line. Clem and Ginnie are good people and they trust you, so who knows if they'd press charges if I found you guilty of some type of fraud. But they'd surely fire you."

"Quit using the word *surely*," she spit out. "Last night it was cute. Now it's just pathetic."

"You need to take a breath, Ms. Reed," Joel said. He sat down in the spare chair next to her.

"In fact, we both need to take a breath," he said softly, raking his fingers through his hair as he worked to regain his calm.

"And I need to see that computer."

By the time Joel had finished examining the bank statements, Maribelle had stopped crying, blown her nose and splashed cold water on her face. She had left Joel to sit at the desk alone, but she paced outside the office door, trying to explain to herself why she hadn't noticed the files in the trash before this morning. She replayed recent maneuvers in her head, going step by step over each action she had performed on the computer in the past several days.

The day Joel first asked to see the income and expense reports, she had wanted to delete some of her private files — things she had no business keeping on the work computer, regardless of her personal circumstances.

He had insisted on seeing them because he hadn't trusted her at that time. Maybe he had never really trusted her. He had acted like he wanted to believe her — likely just an act to ensure her cooperation, and so that she would let her guard down — but he nevertheless made her reveal the contents of the files. That was humiliating, so afterward she had immediately dragged those files to the trash … along with … the bank records?

It made sense now.

At least to Maribelle. To Joel, it would sound like a convenient excuse. Because now Joel had lost trust in her — if he ever had it to begin with.

She wasn't even sure whether to approach him with this explanation. She couldn't prove it, so what difference would it make to try to explain?

The staff would be arriving soon, so she needed to get Joel out of the office. Or maybe it didn't matter now. If he suspected her of wrongdoing, there would be no need to keep the investigation a secret from the staff. Joel would alert Ginnie, Ginnie would fire her — or have her arrested — and they'd promote Bethany to store manager, right before Christmas.

"I'm going for a walk. Lock the back door when you leave," Maribelle told Joel. She already had her coat and gloves on.

Joel looked up, surprised, but she was gone before he could say anything.

21

Maribelle tried to keep the tears from flowing as she stumbled along Bailey Street.

Good thing she had walked this route a million times, or she would have been lost.

She felt lost.

Her heart ached. It ached for Clem, for Ginnie, for the store and its employees, for Joel, for herself. For what might be ... and for what might have been.

The store might be in serious financial trouble. So far not one vendor had taken legal action — at least there was no evidence of that in the metal tin — but that didn't mean they wouldn't. Only time would tell, and they seemed to be running out of time.

Clem might have a serious condition. Time, and probably lots of medical tests, would tell for sure.

Ginnie might have to navigate all these problems alone. Without Clem, without Maribelle, without a staff of people who were loyal to her, if there was no store to keep them employed.

Maribelle might die of a broken heart.

She had really thought Joel was different. Apparently, though, it was all an act. He was staying in her good graces so that she'd trust him enough to reveal something that would help him solve the store's mystery.

Did he even care about Clem and Ginnie? He said he did, but maybe he just wanted the paycheck — or to indulge his intellect by solving an intriguing puzzle. He was supposed to be on "light duty" at his accounting firm; maybe his pay had been cut until he could take on a bigger workload again. Maybe ...

Maybe Maribelle's imagination was running wild again.

Except for the broken heart, all these scenarios would seem ridiculous to a clear mind.

She knew that innocent people went to prison all the time, that employers fired workers for misunderstandings, that health problems manifest in crazy ways before they were brought under control.

But lovers' quarrels seemed to be in a category all their own.

They weren't even lovers, though. They hadn't even spoken the L word. Maribelle had been too afraid.

Now she knew why. It wasn't meant to be. She had stopped it before it could get started.

Before Joel could break her heart.

But he just had.

✳ ✳ ✳

Joel wasn't sure what had just happened.

One minute, he and Maribelle were texting each other silly memes and smiley faces, and the next they were shouting at each other about bank statements and deleted spreadsheets.

Why had he accused her? Why had he jumped to the conclusion that she had manipulated the situation to make herself look innocent? He had found nothing amiss in the bank statements just now. He had even examined the file info and determined that the files were created over the entire year, not in the past few days. The file history showed no modifications since the dates they were created. Nothing amiss.

So, what had happened with him?

He wasn't sure why his reaction had been over the top, but he regretted how he had handled it.

He had made her cry.

Before he left the Bedford Books office, Joel knelt by the office chair and closed his eyes.

"Father, I just screwed up — royally. Maybe it was a subconscious attempt to scare her away. We were getting so close, Father. Was I just afraid of my feelings for her? Help me sort out my feelings, Father, and help me make amends to Maribelle. Father … I love her."

Joel couldn't believe those words had come out of his mouth. He had said them out loud. He opened his eyes and looked to the doorway, hoping Maribelle had come back from her walk, but no one was there.

A sense of peace washed over Joel.

He was going to find Maribelle, apologize and ask her forgiveness.

He'd ask her to let him start fresh with her.

He wanted to court her.

No matter what the future held — with Bedford Books, with Clem and Ginnie, with Maribelle's struggles to trust — he wanted to be with her.

He loved her.

✳ ✳ ✳

By the time Maribelle returned to the store, Joel had locked the back door and left. Bethany was just arriving when Maribelle stomped the snow off her boots and entered.

"Hey, Mare. Where've you been?" Bethany said. "I was worried something had happened."

Bethany looked more closely at Maribelle's face.

"Something *has* happened — you've been crying! What's wrong?"

"I'm just worried about Clem," Maribelle lied. Well, it wasn't a complete lie, but it wasn't what had made her face all red and puffy. Joel was responsible for that.

"Maribelle, someone needs to tell me what's going on with Clem and Ginnie," Bethany said. "He's been AWOL all week, and she has seemed too frantic to talk."

"I'm sorry, Bethany. I know Ginnie has wanted to let everyone know what's going on, but she's not even sure. I'm not at liberty to share anything she has confided in me, but I'll see if she'll give me permission to give everyone an update. Bottom line, though, is that Clem hasn't been himself and Ginnie's trying to get some answers. They're supposed to be seeing his doctor first thing this morning."

"Wow," Bethany said. "I know there's more to the story or you wouldn't have been crying, but I won't pry. I'll wait for you to talk to Ginnie and then tell us."

"The stress of the holiday season on top of Clem's health situation, plus the store's ..." Maribelle bit her tongue. She had almost said too much.

Joel and her employers had not decided to tell the staff about the financial situation — yet. The time would surely come soon, but it wasn't her decision. Especially now that Joel suspected her.

Surely.

She had accused Joel of using that word gratuitously this morning, after their playful use of it last night and in their early-morning text messages.

She felt guilty.

She was guilty. Not of financial misdeeds but of emotional ones.

She had overreacted to Joel's accusations, let her emotions take over and ruined any chance she had of proving she wasn't trying to steal from Bedford Books. She hadn't helped her case by starting to bawl and running out on Joel.

Things would never be the same between them. He didn't trust her anymore — if he ever did — and she wasn't sure that would ever change.

She had blown it.

* * *

Before Maribelle could start wallowing in self-pity, her cell phone rang.

"Dear, we're heading to the doctor's office. I just wanted to ask you to pray for us. Pray that we get some answers."

"I'm already on it, my friend. I've been praying for two days, ever since you called me about Clem."

"You are a precious gift, Maribelle. I love you."

"I love you, too, Ginnie. And Ginnie?"

"Yes, my dear."

Maribelle wanted to tell her employer about her fight with Joel that morning, but she decided she'd save it for later. One burden at a time.

"Give Clem a hug for me."

"I'll give him two — one for you and one for Joel; you seem to be quite a team."

Maribelle hung up before the river of tears could start flowing again.

* * *

As soon as she was off the phone, Maribelle went into the office and closed the door. Stepping over that same strand of Christmas lights they still hadn't hung on the tree — or put away — she headed straight for Clem's office chair.

But instead of sitting in it, she knelt in front of it. She put her elbows on the cool green leather seat, folded her hands and put her head down, eyes closed.

"Father, I'm coming to you again looking for help. Clem needs you. We need you. I need you. We're all helpless on our own, and we know that only you can make sense out of everything that's happening.

We're scared, frustrated ... and, at least in my case, lashing out at the people we love."

Love.

She loved Joel.

The realization hit her hard.

It was probably too little, too late, but she needed to own up to it.

She was in love with Joel Stewart. Tall, dark, handsome, intelligent, kind, wise, frustrating Joel Stewart.

And he was suspicious of her.

She had screwed things up royally.

How could she fix it? Could it be fixed?

She lowered her head again, closed her eyes one more time.

"Father, I'm so selfish. You know that. But right now I want to pray first and foremost for Clem and Ginnie. Make their love STRONG — strong enough to weather whatever storm may come their way. You're the one who calms storms, Father. Calm their hearts of anything that threatens to make them anxious or afraid. Be their peace. Remind them of your gentle and powerful love.

"And, Father, I don't deserve it, but help me make things right with Joel. Help me put my pain, regret and bitterness in the past. Joel doesn't deserve my baggage, and my defensive attitude isn't honoring to you. I ask you to help me gain Joel's trust again. Help him to forgive me. I should've asked you first to forgive me, so I'm doing that now. Forgive me, Father, and heal my heart so that I can fully serve you and live out my purpose. And so that I can love Joel completely. In your Son's name I pray, amen."

Maribelle wiped tears, but this time, instead of tears of anger and hurt, they were tears of joy.

No matter how Joel reacted to her when they saw each other again, she would have joy.

She might not win back his trust and affection, but somehow she would have joy.

And she would start singing Christmas songs again — out loud, so people would hear the good news that had come to the universe so long ago.

And it was still good news today.

✳ ✳ ✳

Maribelle hadn't believed in Santa since she was a child, but she was starting to believe in Christmas miracles again.

And Bethany's sudden appearance in the bookstore's office was about to solve one Christmas mystery for Maribelle, and she would consider it a miracle, too.

"Hey, Beebs. What's up?"

"I see you found the gift," she said.

"Gift?" Maribelle said. "What gift?"

"Well, unless Santa's reindeer came and flew him away last night, you found my epic discovery that I left on the desk for you."

"OH, BETHANY!"

Maribelle flew at her friend and nearly tackled her to the ground with a hug. This time she managed to avoid tripping over the strand of lights.

"So *you're* the reason I was so freaked out last night!" Maribelle laughed. "I thought Santa had come back to haunt me!"

"Haha! You told me no suspense novels, but I didn't think Santa Claus would freak you out! Sorry about that," Bethany said. "No, I searched online for a Santa like Clem's broken dude. It took me awhile to find him, but I couldn't believe how similar he was."

"Actually, I think he was an exact replica. It's hard to tell now that the original is smashed to bits, but I'm pretty sure it's the same Santa ... well, his twin brother, anyway. Only DNA testing could tell us for sure."

Bethany laughed.

"I thought I was busted the other day when you caught me in here writing down some info on Jolly Old St. Nick," she said with a grin.

"So that's what you were doing!" Maribelle laughed. "It all makes sense now! When I saw you whirl around and try to cram something into your pocket nonchalantly, I had a feeling you were up to something, but I sure wasn't thinking about Santa Claus!"

"Oh, Bethany, thank you for Creepy Santa. You're the best!"

While the two stood smiling at each other as old friends do, lightness began to creep back into Maribelle's heart.

Now if they could solve the bookkeeping mystery ... and if Joel could forgive her ... life would take on bright colors again.

22

By the time Maribelle tracked down Joel — without calling him first — he was standing with a beautiful, stylishly dressed redhead in the reception area of Goldman & Blackburn Accounting.

They were standing close to each other, heads down, practically cheek to cheek.

She had her hand on his left arm.

Because his back was to the door, Joel didn't see Maribelle slip in. Neither did anyone else.

She stood for a minute, trying to discern what he and the beautiful woman were saying in such low tones, then she turned around and left silently.

* * *

Thinking foolishly that food might console her, Maribelle was almost to the diner to pick up some lunch when her phone rang. When she looked at the screen, she realized she had a missed call and made a mental note to check her voicemail after she answered Ginnie's incoming call.

Putting the phone on speaker, she answered her employer.

"How's Clem?" she said without even greeting Ginnie. Sometimes she could kick herself for skipping formalities, but she knew Ginnie would overlook it.

"They're scheduling all kinds of tests," Ginnie said. "They've done some quick evaluations and weren't thrilled with what they found. However, they see no reason to admit him to the hospital, so they're going to do a few more quick assessments this morning and send us home as soon as they have a timeframe for us."

"It's too bad today's Friday," Maribelle said. "I hate that you have to wait and wonder over the weekend."

"Dear, we're not talking about the weekend. It's going to be at least two weeks before he can see any kind of specialist. And some evaluations might not be scheduled for several weeks, depending on what the preliminary tests reveal."

"Oh, my," Maribelle said. "Looks like we have plenty of opportunities to get on our knees."

* * *

After skipping breakfast, Maribelle was so eager to get to the diner to pick up a quick salad that she forgot she had missed a call before she talked to Ginnie.

She took her lunch back to the bookstore and holed up in the office with the door closed. She could use a few minutes to savor a meal before she had to help the rest of the crew with the extra load.

As she crunched on lettuce and other veggies dressed with her favorite balsamic vinaigrette, she breathed a few words of prayer. Her heart was hurting over all that was happening — over all that was to come — but she was determined to maintain a sense of peace and joy, no matter what.

Her heart felt heavy, but part of her new resolve was to show the world that a Christian could still have joy, even when the world seemed to be falling apart around her.

Consider it pure joy, my brothers and sisters, whenever you face trials of many kinds, because you know that the testing of your faith produces perseverance. Let perseverance finish its work so that you may be mature and complete, not lacking anything."

Her dad had taught her those verses from James 1 when she was a teenager, and they had gotten her family through many hardships. She was grateful she had memorized them because the words were coming in really handy these days.

As Maribelle took her last bite of salad, Bethany knocked, then entered Maribelle's quiet sanctuary without invitation.

"Mare, we need you. Adam needs to take a lunch break, and Todd and I are swamped. We've been holding down the fort since we opened this morning. Can you please come and help us?"

"Of course, Bethany. I'm so sorry I haven't been here. I've been struggling with some personal stuff, and I shouldn't have let it keep me from doing my job. I know this is a terrible time for me to have a meltdown, so I decided to take a lunch break and sit by myself while I prayed."

"I'm sorry you're struggling, Maribelle. Maybe you could tell me about it after we close the store tonight — if you want to," Bethany said.

"I'm not sure how much I can tell you, but I appreciate the offer. We definitely need to get together soon. I need to catch up on your life, too, my friend."

"Deal," Bethany said, and the two stepped over the strand of Christmas lights and went out to face the shoppers.

Joel couldn't concentrate on his work. He had left a voicemail for Maribelle when he got to his office, and he figured she was still angry, because she hadn't returned his call. He understood that the bookstore was busy, but it seemed like she could've taken the time to send him a text message, at the very least. Even a "Buzz off, creep" would have let him know her frame of mind. At least he would know where he stood, that she wasn't ready to forgive him. Maybe no answer was his answer, though. Maybe her typical M.O. was to cut ties completely when she had been wronged, no explanation necessary.

He hoped not.

Voicemail wasn't the ideal medium for apologies, but it was all he had right now. He had needed to meet a new client at the office this morning, and because he had spent so much time on the Bedford Books situation already, he couldn't ask any of his colleagues to step in for him — again. Besides, it was so close to Christmas, most of the staff was taking vacation time. The office wasn't officially closed for the holidays, but things had wound way down until the new year.

Joel had bumped his left arm coming through the agency's door that morning, and he thought it was going to cause the still-healing wound to bleed. Kandis saw it happen and immediately went to his aid. No one else seemed to be around the office, and she helped him roll up his sleeve and take a look. Neither of them mentioned the conversation they'd had a few days earlier about their relationship and about God. Joel prayed there would still be an opportunity to do that, and he was grateful that Kandis was still speaking to him after he let her know he wasn't interested in her romantically.

At least one beautiful redhead was still speaking to him.

The strawberry blond beauty he was most interested in — whom he was in love with — might never speak to him again.

He tried not to think about that as he wrote notes summarizing his conversation with the new client. He had become pretty adept at compartmentalizing his feelings — a skill he had picked up while juggling work responsibilities and caring for his ailing mother, especially when she was in the final stages of Alzheimer's.

He thought of his mother, and of Clem.

"Father, if I'm right about Clem's mental condition, please help me be a support to him and Ginnie. And to Maribelle. They're going to need it. Use me, Father, to bless and support them."

Joel had only recently met Maribelle, but he had never known anyone who made him feel the way he felt when he was around her, almost from the start. He had a sense of wanting to protect her ... to make all her troubles lighter, to help her realize how wonderful she was. Even though he had known her for such a short time, he already had the sense that the Lord had brought them together.

Who knew, maybe it was only for this difficult season with Clem. Maybe he'd be there for Clem and Ginnie, and that was all.

But Joel cared for Maribelle so much, he was willing to be there to support her, too, even if she never returned his deeper feelings. It would be enough to show Christ's love to her without expecting anything in return.

Or would it?

He would have to do a lot of praying about that.

He had barely finished that thought when his cell phone rang. As he dug it out of his pocket, he hoped beyond hope that it was Maribelle.

It was Ginnie.

"How's Clem?" he said after greeting her.

"He's fine — for now. Did Maribelle tell you we're scheduled for tests in the next couple of weeks?"

"I haven't talked to Maribelle since this morning. I'm not sure she wants to talk to me, ever again."

"What are you talking about, dear? Of course she wants to talk to you."

"Ginnie, I hurt her pretty badly this morning. I wouldn't blame her if she never wanted to talk to me after this," he said sadly.

"Dear, it can't be that bad. What happened?"

"I practically accused her of hiding evidence from me, and then finding it 'conveniently' so it would cast her in a better light."

"Oh, Joel, I'm sorry."

"Not half as sorry as I am, Ginnie. I don't know what came over me.

It's almost like I was trying to sabotage our relationship."

"Do you ... did you ... *have* a relationship with Maribelle, dear?"

"We were getting closer, and I had told her recently how I feel. She wasn't ready to reciprocate, but I could tell she wanted to. As you probably know, she's been hurt badly, and I think she's still working through that. I was willing to give her all the time she needed to get past the devastation of her broken engagement. But now I've screwed it up, and I don't know why. It's almost like I did it deliberately."

"Maybe you have your own fears, sweetheart," the older woman said gently.

"It would seem so," he said, realization dawning on him. "I think I've let my parents' relationship color my perception of what a truly happy marriage can be."

Joel realized that he had just uttered the word *marriage*. Was he already that much in love with Maribelle?

Yes. She was all he had wanted in a woman. She was the one. He had told Kandis that he hadn't met the woman he wanted to spend his life with. Now he couldn't imagine life without Maribelle, with her straightforward ways, her stunning eyes and even the parts of her that were vulnerable and in need of healing. He wanted to be the one she took a risk with, to be the man she leaned on, and for the two of them to lean on God together.

He wanted to marry her. Wow.

"Young man, you need to have a talk with your beloved Maribelle. You must find a way to make it right. She'll forgive you; I know her well enough to assure you of that. And Joel?"

"Yes, ma'am?"

"If you need my help, I'm here. I'll stay out of it, because the two of you need to work it out on your own, but I'm here for support if you need it."

"Ginnie, you and Clem have been so generous. I don't know how to say thank you."

"You just did, young man," Ginnie said. "Now, I have something else to tell you that may lift your spirits. And perhaps it will help make things easier when you talk to Maribelle."

"What's that, ma'am?"

"Clem brought up the tin of papers when we were on the way home this afternoon."

"What did he say? I'm almost afraid to ask."

"It was as though the subject had never come up and he was informing me of a treasure he had been keeping in the office all this time," Ginnie said.

"He admitted that he put the papers in the tin and hid it away. Only he didn't consider it hiding. He put them there for convenience, and apparently he had been adding to it regularly for months."

"Ginnie, do you realize what this means?" Joel practically shouted.

"I think so. If I'm right, there is no thief in our midst," Ginnie said. "I have an ill husband, whom I'm extremely worried about, but we don't have any criminal activity going on at our store."

"Ginnie, that's tremendous news!" This time Joel did shout, with the unbridled joy of a man suddenly granted a second chance.

He couldn't wait to tell Maribelle.

"And I'm sorry that Clem is experiencing these memory problems," he said. This good news didn't change the fact that Clem was in serious trouble. Joel didn't mention Alzheimer's or dementia again, but he was pretty sure it was only a matter of time before the doctors reached that conclusion.

"It's something we're probably going to have to get used to, Joel, and I've already been talking to the Lord about it. I've asked him to prepare me for what is to come. I've asked him to give us all peace as we work through it."

"I want to be there by your side as you love and support your husband, Ginnie. I'm committed to that, if you'll let me."

"Joel, you're a dear young man. Thank you for how you've already supported us. I know I'll need you, and I accept your help. Maribelle will need you, too. Now, go find your young lady and make things right."

"Yes, ma'am!"

23

Joel couldn't wipe the smile off his face as he raced to Bedford Books, trying not to run any red lights for real this time.

His heart was full, and his thoughts were racing faster than his car's V6 engine.

He knew it might take some convincing to get Maribelle to forgive him for being a jerk, but he was determined to try.

He was sad about his aging friend, no doubt. Clem and Ginnie would face a difficult road in the coming weeks, months and, perhaps, years. But the Lord had sent a glimmer of hope for Joel to cling to as he rushed to tell the woman he loved that he was crazy about her.

If she would accept his apology.

Even if she wasn't willing to forgive, he would make her hear the whole story before she sent him away. He would tell her how he realized he was still holding resentment because of his parents, how he now knew he had unconsciously tried to sabotage his budding relationship with Maribelle … and that, no matter what results he might have discovered in his investigation of Bedford Books, he wanted to be with her.

He wanted her to know that he never really suspected her — that he knew from the beginning that she was a trustworthy person.

What Joel did suspect, though, was that the enemy was trying to drive a wedge between him and Maribelle. Satan was in the business of wrecking relationships, and he would stop at nothing to kill and destroy people's hopes and dreams, to make them turn from God and toward darkness — toward the coward who would never win the war, even though he had seemed to win a lot of skirmishes.

But Joel served a God who was more mighty than the devil, and Joel called on his mighty God's help now.

"Father, soften Maribelle's heart toward me. Help me find the right words to say, so that she'll realize how wonderful she is and how much you love her — how much I love her — and help her accept my apology. Forgive me for the resentment I've been carrying for years. Remove it from me, and replace it with your love and the knowledge that you're all I need. I ask you to give me Maribelle's love and companionship, for the rest of my life — if it's your will."

No matter how Maribelle received Joel's confession and apology, he was determined to tell her every bit of it.

He loved her, and he needed her to know.

No doubt he was uncertain of how she would react, but the silly grin simply refused to leave his face.

He believed that the Lord had brought Maribelle into his life, not only so that they could support Clem and Ginnie together but so that Joel could love her.

So that he could spend the rest of his life with her.

And somehow he would find a way to convince her of that.

✳ ✳ ✳

Joel entered through the front door of the bookstore.

When Maribelle heard the jingle of the little bell on the door, she looked up from the customer she was helping.

Her heart lurched into her throat. She stopped midsentence and couldn't go on. The customer turned to see what had turned Maribelle into a speechless statue, then returned to their conversation.

"Thank you for wrapping the gift so beautifully, young lady. My sister's going to love the elegant silver and purple paper."

"Thank you for shopping at Bedford Books, Mrs. ... umm ..."

"Carter," the customer reminded her. "It's OK, young lady. I can see you have other business to attend to. Go greet your young man," the elderly woman said, her eyes twinkling.

"He's not my young man, ma'am."

"I see," Mrs. Carter said, although Maribelle could tell she was not convinced. "Well, it's only a matter of time. You'll have to tell me about him next time I visit. Merry Christmas!"

"Merry Christmas," Maribelle murmured, without taking her eyes off Joel as he made his way to the counter.

Tears of gratitude welled in her eyes.

The Lord had answered his daughter's prayer. He had given her an opportunity to ask Joel's forgiveness. Even if this beautiful, kind man wanted to be with the gorgeous woman she had seen him with this morning, Maribelle still needed to make things right.

Joel spoke first.

"I know you're busy, and I know you're still angry with me and probably never want to see me again, but if you'd be willing to give me five minutes, I'd like to talk. I need to apologize."

"*You* need to apologize? I'm the one who needs to apologize," Maribelle said. "And I'll give you a lot more than five minutes if you can wait until the store closes. If we can both wait."

"I hate waiting," Joel said with a smile.

"Me, too," she chuckled. "But I think it will be OK now. Now that I've seen your face and know that you don't hate me, I can breathe again."

"I could never hate you, Mare," he said, barely above a whisper.

Why did it send a thrill through her insides to hear him call her by this nickname? It was so endearing, so ... intimate.

"The store closes at 6, and it takes us 30 to 45 minutes to clean up and get things ready for the next day. You want to meet me somewhere after that?"

"I could come by at 6 and help you clean up. Maybe that would make it go by faster."

"You don't have to do that, but we surely won't turn down the help. The Friday before Christmas is our second-busiest day of the year — Saturday being the busiest."

"See you at 5:59."

She almost blew him a kiss, but she restrained herself.

✳ ✳ ✳

At 6:23 p.m., Joel was still nowhere in sight.

Maribelle was trying to keep busy, partly so they could hurry and finish cleaning the store and partly to keep her mind off Joel's noticeable absence. Usually he was punctual to a fault, so why hadn't he made it by now? Had he changed his mind about her? Had he found out new information that implicated her, after all? Maybe it wasn't just Clem's dementia; maybe the bookkeeping mess was still a mess.

Hot news? Cold feet? Which was it?

Or was it something else? But what could it be?

As Maribelle emptied the trash in the large bin across the alley, she willed herself not to cry. Maybe she should stand out here in the biting cold and pull herself together. The chill usually brought clarity to her mind.

But not this time. Too many things had been crowding her thoughts and emotions lately; there was no bandwidth to process this new fear.

Fear.

That's what it was. When she had prayed that morning for the Lord to give her and the others answers today, she certainly hadn't been expecting more *questions*!

But the Lord had not given her a spirit of fear. He gave her a spirit of power, love and self-control. She thanked him for bringing to mind the message in 2 Timothy 1:7, and the tension relaxed its vise grip on her neck and shoulders.

Maybe Joel was hurt. Had he had an accident on the way there?

Immediately she pulled out her cell phone — not to call Joel just yet; that could wait. She launched her interactive Bible and swiped through the books to Psalm 5, the chapter she had read that morning. She prayed a piece of it:

Spread your protection over them,
that all who love your name may be filled with joy.

Maribelle tossed the bag of trash into the bin and turned back toward the bookstore. Once she was inside, away from the cold wind, she closed the door and headed for the office, whispering a prayer as she stepped over the Christmas lights: *Spread your protection over them, heavenly Father.*

✳ ✳ ✳

Joel called from the emergency room.

When Maribelle saw "Harbor Medical Center" on the caller ID, her knees turned to jelly and she lurched for Clem's green office chair. She sat down with a slam and grabbed the receiver, fighting nausea.

"Yes?" she answered. "I mean, Bedford Books, Maribelle speaking."

"Maribelle, it's Joel."

She allowed the dam of emotions to burst.

"Joel, are you all right? Why are you at the hospital?" she demanded through her tears.

"My co-worker Kandis had a car accident this evening on her way home from work. My best friend, Andre, called me and I met them at the ER. Andre works with us, too.

"Is Kandis badly injured?"

"It doesn't appear so. She has a broken arm, but they've already done a CT scan and they don't think she has any damage to her head, neck or lower spine. We're waiting for the radiologist to read it before they release her."

"What can I do?"

"You can forgive me for not showing up at the store. I'm sure you were thinking I had changed my mind."

"Well … the thought did occur to me," she said. "But I've been around you long enough to know that you wouldn't just *not* show up without letting me know — or without good reason."

"You're right, Maribelle. I would never do that to you — or anyone."

She knew this was true, and it made her love him even more.

"Do you need me to come to the hospital?" Maribelle was prepared to offer Todd or Bethany double pay — out of her own pocket — to stay extra late and finish up so she could leave. She wanted that badly to see Joel.

"I think we'll be on our way home with Kandis by the time you could get here. Andre and I are going to take her home and get her settled in tonight, and I don't know how long it will take. Can we have our conversation tomorrow?"

"Of course, Joel. The store closes at 7, though. Last Saturday before Christmas, we always close late."

"I understand. I'll call you in the morning, and we'll figure it out. I need to get off the phone now. I had to call from the waiting room because my cell battery's drained."

"Well, that explains it. Seeing the hospital's name on the caller ID took at least 10 years off my life!"

"Sorry, Mare. I would've used Andre's cell, but he was calling our boss to let her know about Kandis, and I didn't want to wait one more minute to talk to you."

"I forgive you, Joel," she said with a grin that he could hear through the phone line.

He smiled and said goodnight.

✳ ✳ ✳

"You up?" Joel texted early the next morning.

Maribelle: Dickens was hungry I've been up for an hour woke up to

143

cat eyeballs three inches from my face LOL

Joel: Haha! What a rude awakening, huh? I've been up since sunrise but was afraid to text you too early. Shirley's already had her breakfast, too. :)

Maribelle: How are things today have you heard from your friend Candace?

Joel: Andre texted me after she called him this morning. Her arm's aching, but she said she's OK. She's taking a hiatus from text messaging for a while. :)

Maribelle: Are you going to need to help her out today

Joel: Kandi's mom and brother live in town, so between them and Andre, she should be taken care of. I'll check in on her, of course. Besides being co-workers, we're friends.

Maribelle: Youre a good friend :)

Joel: Listen, Mare, I know this is late notice, but with everything that's been going on, I had completely forgotten about our work Christmas party tonight. Is there any chance you'd be able to go with me? I'm not in the habit of asking for dates at the last minute, or by text message, but I thought you might make an exception. (Insert irresistible smile from charming accountant.)

Maribelle: LOL what time does it start is it formal how many people will be there

Joel: Starts at 7:30, won't last more than an hour, it's Christmas-casual (whatever that means), and it's just the office staff and their significant others. No kids, because most of the staff is single or newly married. We usually have appetizers, exchange inexpensive gifts, hug each other and go our separate ways. It sounds kind of pathetic, but it's a small way to show each other we care when we're not buried in spreadsheets and audits. We're so scattered during the week, we started having it after hours at Kim's house. (She's our boss.)

Was she Joel's "significant other"? She had fixated on that phrase and hadn't comprehended one bit of the rest of Joel's paragraph. She would love to have a conversation about that right now, but she had to get ready for work. It would have to wait.

Maribelle: I'd love to go, but I'll have to drink something stronger than peppermint tea to pep me up at the end of the day. Maybe I'll have an espresso!

Joel: Haha! I'll make sure Kim has some on hand. I'll let you go, but text me today if you get a minute. I want to know how your day's going. And let me know if you hear from Ginnie.

Maribelle: Will do have a great day

Joel: You, too, Maribelle. :)

Patience, Joel, he told himself.

With that last sentence, instead of "Maribelle" he had wanted to say "my love," but he needed to take one step at a time. No use scaring her off before he'd had a chance to say the words to her face.

✳ ✳ ✳

Midday, Maribelle realized she needed to provide a hostess gift to Joel's boss tonight. She had forgotten to ask him about it in the morning, so she decided this would be a good time to text him.

Maribelle: Does Kim like to read? I'd like to give her a book

Joel: You don't have to do that.

Maribelle: I know but you didn't answer my question :)

Joel: Yes, she does. I've seen books in her office. I think her favorite author is Terry B.... Terry Something. She writes mystery-suspense type books. Strong women, according to the boss lady.

Maribelle: Terri Blackstock

Joel: Yes, that's it!

Maribelle: We have her latest in stock I'll wrap it up

Joel: You're a good egg.

Maribelle: Slightly scrambled but those are the best kind, right

Joel: ☺ I look forward to tonight.

Maribelle: Me too

As Maribelle straightened the chairs in the children's section, she found herself humming, "Oh, tidings of comfort and joy ..."

* * *

The store was surprisingly slow at the end of the day, so the crew decided to close up at 6:50 and save the tidying up for Sunday afternoon. Maribelle planned to stop by after church and put things in order for Monday.

By the time Joel rang her doorbell, she was outfitted in her favorite emerald-green silk sweater with an off-white pencil skirt and beige pumps. The stress of the past few weeks had played havoc on her appetite, so, to her delight, she was able to squeeze into the skirt again. She just wouldn't have any dessert tonight, she promised herself.

She had put her hair up, with soft tendrils curling around her face, and she completed the look with a pair of crystal and pearl snowflake earrings. The green of the sweater set off her beautiful strawberry-blond hair and made her usually pale blue eyes look aqua tonight.

When Maribelle opened the door, Joel took one look at her and stared, speechless for a moment.

"Wow."

"Do I look OK?" Judging by his reaction, the question was gratuitous, but she couldn't resist asking it.

"You look fantastic."

"Thank you," Maribelle said. "You clean up nice, yourself." He was wearing a charcoal gray sport coat and slacks with a light gray pin-stripe shirt and a purple silk tie — one she hadn't seen before.

They stared at each other for a lingering moment, then Maribelle broke the spell by turning to grab her coat and the gift bag she had sitting by the door.

* * *

Arriving at Kim's, Maribelle felt a sudden surge of uncertainty, making her stomach turn somersaults.

Was this their first date? *Was* it a date? What had Joel told his boss about her? Would she be welcomed by his co-workers?

But let all who take refuge in you rejoice;
let them sing joyful praises forever.

Remembering the Psalms she had been reading, she let her neck and shoulders relax. The Lord's opinion of her was all that mattered. She cared what Joel thought, too, but even his opinion was secondary to the Lord's. If she behaved according to the Holy Spirit's leading, she'd be fine.

Joel parked the car, then went around to Maribelle's door and opened it for her as a light snow fell. "Need me to grab that bag for you?" he offered.

"No, thanks. Just need one gift out of it. The rest can stay in the car."

Joel grabbed his own gift bag from the back seat and helped Maribelle out before locking the car doors.

"Come in!" Kim said, grabbing Maribelle's hand and leading her into the foyer of her house.

"You must be Maribelle. I'm Kim," she said warmly as she took Maribelle's red coat and scarf.

So Joel had told Kim about her. OK.

Joel led her into the living room and began introductions.

"Andre, I'd like you to meet Maribelle," he said as his best friend turned around.

The good-looking dark-skinned man was almost as tall as Joel, and almost as handsome. He walked over and shook Maribelle's hand.

"It's very nice to meet you, Maribelle. I'm so glad you came."

The woman Andre had been speaking to turned around, too, and Maribelle almost fainted.

It was the beautiful redhead Joel had been chatting so intimately with at his office the other morning.

"Hi, I'm Kandis," she said, extending her left hand. "I'm afraid I can't shake with my right. I broke my arm last night."

Maribelle forced a smile, but her insides wanted to let out a scream.

"Nice to meet you; I'm sorry about your arm," she managed to say. "Joel told me about your accident; I hope you're OK."

"I'll be fine as long as I can hold onto a shred or two of dignity. It's a bit humiliating to ask your mother to help you dress for a party. Besides, with friends like the ones in this room, I'm a blessed woman."

"Indeed," Maribelle mumbled. "With Joel and Andre around, what more could you ask?"

"I agree!" she said, giving Andre a shy smile. "Joel's going to get payback for asking me to help him with his sutures the other day. I'm extremely squeamish at the sight of blood, but there was no one else in the office when he bumped his injured forearm. I had to roll up his sleeve and help him stop the bleeding. It's a wonder I didn't pass out. Yes, you owe me, friend!" Kandis laughed, giving Joel a teasing look.

Maribelle let out a long, slow breath, and when Kim came around to take drink orders, Joel's date was completely relaxed.

24

Joel opened Maribelle's car door and waited until she was comfortably inside with her seatbelt on, then he closed the door and went around to his side.

Once he was buckled in and had started the engine to get the heater going, he turned to Maribelle and said, "I have a gift for you, but I'd like to go somewhere warm so we can sit and talk without our teeth chattering."

"How about Difalso's?" she suggested.

"Perfect!"

Joel put the car in gear and headed for the Italian restaurant where he and Maribelle had first let their guard down with each other.

* * *

The same waiter who had served them the first time was on the spot as soon as they got settled into the booth in the back corner. But this time, instead of sitting across from each other, Joel and Maribelle slid into the same side of the booth. Their legs were close enough to touch.

"It is exquisite to see you both again, my friends! What may I bring you to drink?"

"Need that espresso yet?" Joel teased Maribelle.

"Not yet. You'll know if I start yawning midsentence."

"OK, just checking. I thought maybe that's why you recommended Difalso's."

She looked at him, and his grin left her in a puddle. Maribelle felt warm and happy, and she suspected that she'd have sweet dreams tonight.

Joel ordered two ice waters for them, and they watched the waiter disappear to the kitchen.

He turned toward her in the booth, his right arm behind her on the back of the seat. His knee bumped hers, and he left it there, sending an electrical current through her entire body.

"Maribelle, I've been dying to talk to you since our fight."

"Me, too. I can't believe how I overreacted, Joel."

"You? I'm the one who overreacted."

She laid her hand on his left forearm, and this time he was the one who felt the shockwave.

"Listen," he said gently. "I don't need to tell you that the stress level has been sky high lately. There's the bookkeeping situation, Clem's health, the resurrection of crazy Santa from the dead ..."

"Oh, yeah, I meant to tell you about Santa," Maribelle interrupted. "Bethany remembered seeing a Santa that was a lot like Clem's in her parents' attic, and she wanted to bring him to the store after hearing how crushed I was — no pun intended — for breaking Clem's Santa Claus. She didn't find her parents' Santa, but that made her even more determined. She went online and found him.

"It was just like Bethany to go to all that trouble for someone she cares about. She didn't mean to creep me out, but she did get a wicked thrill out of it when I told her about my over-the-top reaction. It was another example of my overreacting to something completely innocent, which just goes to show I need a vacation!

"And I'm very, very sorry, Joel."

"Maribelle, we both overreacted, and I'm sorry, too. I'll forgive you if you'll forgive me."

"Deal."

He looked into her eyes and moved his face closer to hers.

"Your water, my friends!" the smiling waiter said.

"Grazi, signore."

"Prego. Have you decided on your meals?"

The young couple exchanged a look. They hadn't even opened their menus. They had eaten appetizers at Kim's, and neither was very hungry. But there was always room for dessert.

"How about a double-dark-chocolate cake, to split?" Maribelle said. "I promise I won't spear your hand with my fork."

"Sounds perfect. One plate, two forks," he told the waiter.

"Very good, signore and signora. I'll be back in a flash, as they say!"

"Take your time," Joel said to the waiter's back.

Maribelle laughed and turned back to her companion.

"Joel, it's strange. No, now that I think about it, *strange* isn't the right word. Disappointment is what I feel after having our argument. I had just sat in my room and prayed an hour earlier that the Lord would give us answers and that I would love my people well, no matter what."

"Gosh, that's almost exactly what I prayed that morning."

"The enemy sure knows how to push our buttons. Sometimes it makes me wonder if prayer even works," she said. "But I know that's not true. I know that as soon as we take our eyes off Jesus and focus on ourselves, we can get off track in a flash."

"I think that happened to both of us," Joel said. "And, on that note, how about we pray about it right now?"

They bowed their heads and asked for daily reminders of how much they needed the Lord's grace, guidance and forgiveness. When they finished praying, they resolved to hold each other accountable.

The double-dark-chocolate cake had appeared silently on the table while their eyes were closed.

"This goes great with espresso," Maribelle said.

Joel raised his eyebrows.

"I thought you were joking about espresso this morning," he said.

"No, actually I love coffee — the darker the better," she smiled. "And I've always enjoyed espresso for celebrations. I drink it when I'm happy, but I haven't had an occasion to celebrate in a long time."

You would think she'd just told him she liked to take a nip of arsenic after a good meal.

He finally spoke.

"I thought *peppermint tea* was your drink of choice."

"Actually … I have a confession." she said with a sheepish smile. "I really kind of force myself to drink peppermint tea."

"WHAT? You've got to be kidding me!" Joel looked around, embarrassed at his outburst, then lowered his voice. "You drink peppermint tea by the gallon!"

She took a deep breath, then prepared to explain.

"Well, it does settle my stomach when I'm nervous. But I only started drinking it after reading a novel in which the main character, a novelist, drank peppermint tea. It's kind of embarrassing to admit, but I only drink it because it makes me feel like an author.

"Of course I've written about two sentences in my novel so far, so I'm not even close to being an author. I probably never will be."

Joel looked like he was in shock.

"It's OK. You don't have to keep it a secret," she said. "Now that

I've finally told someone, I can stop drinking it. It was a pretentious, silly thing to do, and I'm over it."

"It's not that," Joel said, finally able to speak.

"Then what?"

He pulled out the gift he had carried in from the car.

"Open it."

Underneath the beautiful red-and-white striped wrapping paper was a wooden box a little smaller than the metal tin where Clem kept his documents. Maribelle opened it and gasped.

Then she laughed out loud, and nearby diners looked up from their food.

It was a tea box, and inside was an assortment of loose-leaf teas, all peppermint-flavored.

"Oh, Joel, this is the best gift ever!" she exclaimed.

"Really? I was thinking just the opposite, after what you just told me."

She reached under the table for the gift she had carried in. She handed it to Joel and said, "Open yours. And don't try to save the wrapping paper. I have more. Just tear into it!"

Now it was Joel's turn to laugh.

His box contained a pair of handmade purple socks, knitted by the woman sitting next to him.

"I'm going to get you a real gift next week — one that's any color but purple," she said. "I didn't know about your purple aversion when Dickens and I were working on these, but I haven't had time to shop lately. I've had to deal with this annoying audit that's taken every spare minute of my time."

"Don't you dare shop for another gift!" Joel said. "These will be perfect for sitting in front of the fire watching movies as I snuggle with the woman of my dreams — and her cat."

"And your dog."

"It will be quite the little domestic scene," Joel said.

Then he turned to face Maribelle full on, gently tracing her jaw with his finger. As his face grew serious, he looked straight into her eyes and said the words he had been longing to say out loud for days.

"I love you, Maribelle."

Tears welling in her eyes, she said, "I've been waiting to hear you say those words to me. ... I love you, too, my beautiful Joel."

Then, looking around to be sure the waiter was staying occupied with the other diners, Joel leaned in, held Maribelle's face in his hands and gently kissed her. A kiss that would have made her tingle all the

way down to her purple socks, if she had been wearing any.
"I'm ready for my espresso now."

✳ ✳ ✳

**Want to find out what happens next with Andre and Kandis?
Subscribe to my newsletter just for book lovers:**
https://suzyoakley.com/books

Thank you!

All honor and glory to my Savior, Jesus Christ. Without you, I can do nothing. May these words bring people to you.

✵ ✵ ✵

So many people helped me realize my dream of publishing my first book, and no words could adequately say thank you to:

Mom, for bearing with me through ... well, everything.

Bruce, for putting up with me, for reading a book in a genre you "don't get," and for the editing, proofreading and wordsmithing. When I met you in that newsroom 25 years ago, who knew we'd make such a team?

Anna Huckabee, for the weekly FaceTime chats where we hold each other accountable and where you lift me up with your wisdom, experience and encouragement. Thanks for reminding me that I don't have to follow the crowd. (And thanks for beta-reading.)

Kirsten Oliphant and the Create If Writing community. Wow. Y'all are like family to me.

Pamela Hill, my cousin, BFF, sister in Christ and accountability partner. We've been through a lot together. I love you to pieces.

My awesome beta readers: **Annette Edwards, Barb and Brian Pope**, **Patty Scott, Kathy Skinner** and **Anna Huckabee**.

✵ ✵ ✵

A true friend is one who doesn't let you settle for the status quo simply because it's easier. She doesn't accept your excuses; she pushes you to find a better way when you're tempted to settle for one that's "acceptable." Barb, you've always been that friend for me in life, and with this book, you became so in my writing, too.

Patty, you went above and beyond your assigned duties as a beta reader. You took the time to make suggestions and additions that made the book better. I can never thank you enough.

Let's do this again soon, OK?

Made in the USA
Columbia, SC
23 December 2019